Deep Gold

A Chase Gordon Tropical Thriller

Douglas Pratt

MANTA PRESS

Deep Gold is a work of fiction. Any names, places, characters, and incidents are products of the author's imagination or are used fictitiously. Any resemblance to actual persons, either living or dead, events, or locales is entirely coincidental.

For Ashlee

January 3, 1941

Waves lapped against the wooden hull. A soft wind carried the sound of the ocean through the night air. The tilted moon smiled down on the dark sea but refused to illuminate the water, forcing the man to rely on the soft, yellow glow from the kerosene lanterns hanging over the helm.

The fish had been active. Twisdale Altman had reeled in two big tarpon and a medium-sized tuna; those were happy bonuses. He was counting on another hefty shrimp pull. The locker was half-full of prawns. They were still running, which was an unusual blessing. Usually by the end of December, he'd have to pick through the estuaries to get a decent haul. Tonight, he just happened upon a large school, and if he could pull in another full net or two, he'd have an excellent start to the year.

"Jacob," the man shouted at the boy manning one of the lines, "you got something."

The little brown-haired boy snapped out of his half-doze. He grabbed the rod and began pumping his arm as he tried to reel in the catch.

"Slow down, boy," his father warned him. "You'll tire yourself out before you will the fish."

"Sorry, Pop," the nine-year-old apologized.

Twisdale's smile caught the glow of the lantern as he watched his boy struggle to hold on to the pole. It was too big for him, but Twisdale wanted him to feel the thrill of pulling his own catch. The arch of the rod told Twisdale it was a small one. Enough for the boy to feel his heart race without the worry of losing the rod to the sea.

"Remember," Twisdale pointed out, "don't let the line have too much slack. Keep it tight."

His teeth tightened on his lip as he tried to follow his father's instructions, Jacob nodded into the dark. To an observer, the boy was thinking as he made deliberate moves. Things that he had watched his father do. His leather boots were square and perpendicular to the gunwale of the boat as the little fisherman grasped the rod and heaved back, trying not to let the fish pull him as it fought to break free.

Twisdale wanted to watch Jacob haul in what he suspected was a small dolphinfish. Maybe a tuna. It would be a treat for Jacob to take home his catch to his mother. She'd praise him and fry it up with some hushpuppies.

The line on the net was taut, and he needed to get it aboard. This second haul was heavy, and he wondered if a large fish had gotten entwined in the net. He cranked the winch on the stern of the boat. The gears clicked slowly as he struggled to hoist the net. This wasn't just shrimp in the catch. The davit hanging over the vessel's stern creaked and groaned as the cable wound around the winch's barrel.

The flash of white caught his eye, but without the moonlight, he couldn't tell what was in the net. The back of his mind warned him that it was a shark. It wasn't unusual to snag a bull shark going after his catch, but he'd never tangled one up in a net.

His hand wrapped around a gaff, and he stretched the hook toward the line. He didn't want to lose the net and cable, but it wasn't designed for several hundred pounds. Whatever it was, it wasn't thrashing like a shark might.

He pulled the cable toward him. If he could get it closer to the stern rail, he could see what he snagged.

"Jacob!," the man yelled forward. "Cut the engine!"

The boy glanced at his line, still twanging in the night. He released the reel, giving his catch the slack to take a break. After securing the rod, he ran to the helm and pulled the throttle back. The engine was barely trolling along, but as soon as the vessel's forward momentum stopped, Twisdale could bring the net closer.

"Damn," the fisherman whispered under his breath.

The face of a man stared up at him. Twisdale sucked in a breath when the face blinked. He was alive.

"Jacob! My knife!"

The boy pulled a four-inch blade from the sheath hanging on the helm. Realizing his father's distress, Jacob ran aft carrying the knife. Usually, that would have garnered a stern discussion about safety. He stretched out his hand, turning the knife so that the handle was pointing at Twisdale. When Jacob saw a man wrapped in the twine of the shrimp net, he jumped back, scared.

Ignoring his son's fear, his father snatched the handle from the boy. With one hand, Twisdale held the weight of the man in the net out of the water as he weaved the blade under the cotton strands and cut the net open.

The knife slipped along the net, spilling the contents. The boy thought it reminded him of gutting a big fish.

"Here." Twisdale dropped the knife and grabbed the man by the front of his shirt. He heaved him back, pulling him up and over the railing.

A gaunt man sprawled on the deck of the boat. A wooden box fell from his arms. His upper body heaved up and down as he tried to breathe.

"Get a coat," the fisherman ordered Jacob. "Hurry."

The boy scampered into the cabin.

"Mister, are you alright?"

The stranger on the deck shifted, offering a groan in response to Twisdale's question. Hooking his arms under the near-drowned man, the short fisherman rolled him onto his back. The stars held his gaze for a second as the man attempted to put some weight on his elbow.

He was wearing some type of gray coveralls. The name "Vogel" stitched into the left chest.

"Is your name Vogel?" Twisdale asked.

The blue eyes widened at the question, and slowly he shook his head.

Jacob returned with a leather jacket that Alice made Twisdale several years earlier. He took the coat from his son and draped it around the stranger's shoulders.

"Jacob," his father commanded, "go check the lines."

When the boy vanished into the dark again, he looked at the drenched man. "What's your name?"

"Richman," the man grunted through shivering lips. "Henry Richman."

"I have some stew," Twisdale offered. "I doubt it's still hot."

Richman's head nodded with considerable effort.

"Can you stand?"

"I think I can," Richman answered. His words were slow and deliberate.

Twisdale draped an arm around Richman and helped him get to his feet. Richman paused, putting a hand on the rail to balance himself. His eyes moved across the deck to the wooden box lying on its side.

The fisherman didn't speak. Instead, he studied the box for a split second. It wasn't much bigger than a tackle box. It had a hasp that secured it shut.

"Come on over here," he urged Richman toward a bench along the starboard side.

The man shook as he dripped on the deck, but he seemed to be gaining some strength.

"Rest here," Twisdale told him. "I'll get you some stew."

When he returned, he found Richman on the bench with the wooden box resting beside him. He handed a wooden bowl with some cold stew to the shivering man.

"Sorry, I don't have a spoon."

"Thank you." Richman muttered through chattering teeth as he took the bowl. He scooped up the chunks of meat with two fingers and shoveled it into his mouth.

"What happened to you? Where did you come from?"

With his mouth full, Richman responded, "I was on a small boat. A wave flipped it over."

"How long have you been out there?"

He shook his head as if he didn't know the answer.

"Take your time. You're safe now," Twisdale assured Richman, who nodded appreciatively.

"I got to pull the net in, and we'll get you to shore."

Richman remained silent as he scooped more stew into his mouth. Twisdale walked over to Jacob, trying to reel in his line again, hoping that his catch hadn't made an escape during the commotion.

"Jacob, pull in all the lines," he ordered, "and get in the cabin and start cleaning those tarpon."

"Why the cabin?" the boy asked.

"Just do it," he reiterated. "We got to get that man to shore."

"Yes, Pop."

Twisdale reached over the stern rail and found the ruined net. He guessed it would cost him one of those tarpons to get it repaired. Any shrimp caught up in it found their release when he cut Richman out of it. At least the first haul he pulled in would make up for losing the net.

With the net hauled aboard and tied off, Twisdale started the little motor and pushed the throttle forward. He checked his watch before taking a bearing from the compass. He steered the boat northwest by 12 degrees.

From the helm, he could see Richman, who looked as if he was passed out. The cold and exhaustion overcame him, and Twisdale considered how lucky this man was.

In the shadows, Richman was resting, but he wasn't asleep. Instead, he was fondling a coin in his hand. Keeping the back of his hand toward the fisherman, he ran his fingers over the markings. When the captain's attention shifted elsewhere, the man slipped the gold coin under the bench. He had no intention of staying around long when they reached shore, but he felt a kindness for a kindness was due.

1

The sand was scorching, baking in the Florida sun. White surf rolled onto the beach. A foaming tongue from the sea licked at my feet as I stared at the clouds dancing overhead. Orange embers in the pit murmured as their heat spread to the driftwood I just added.

Salty water was drying off my skin. I'd just waded ashore with a fresh catch. The yellow-tail snapper hung limp on the end of my speargun.

This little patch of sand and grass had been my home for the last two days. *Carina,* my 40-foot Tartan sailboat, sat at anchor in the harbor of a bigger island. I wanted to get a little primitive, a feat for someone that lives every day in less than 300 square feet. There was nothing special about this particular island. With over 1,700 islands in the Florida Keys, it was easy to find a quiet and uninhabited piece of land.

Beth, my wooden dinghy, rested on the sand above the high tide line. An empty hammock stretched between two small trees just past the beach. I learned my lesson when

I first moved to Florida. The mosquitoes and bugs were ravenous. They made their home among the mangroves. It took one camping trip to realize my hammock needed mosquito netting if I didn't want to donate a significant portion of my blood to the little vampires. During the day, the bugs stayed close to the shade. As long as I stayed in the sun, I found safety.

There was no schedule. My life right now paid little heed to the hands of any clock. Most days I lived on *Carina*, sailing to whatever spot offered the best snorkeling or diving. When my supplies ran dry, I'd head back to port and try to make a little money to survive a few more months at sea. Right now, though, my coffers were full. Over-filled. I wouldn't have to get behind the bar and sling drinks for quite a while. Which leaves me plenty of time for camping in the open air, counting stars, and spearfishing.

Pulling myself up into a seated position, I prepped my lunch. The snapper I speared a few minutes ago was close to a three-pounder. Way more than enough for me to eat for lunch. With my fillet knife, I sliced through the meat as close to the thin bones as possible. The first few times I tried to fillet a fish, I ended up with a pile of meat. Now after a few years of practice, I can usually pull a solid fillet. Next, I cut two long strips with the skin still on one side that I rested on top of the fresh driftwood. From a shaker filled with garlic and Cajun seasonings, I sprinkled a dusting over each fillet.

The fish wouldn't take long to cook. Five minutes, tops. Much more, and the meat will start to dry out.

While the coals worked the meat, I grabbed a jug of water that I buried up to its neck. The sand worked as an excellent insulator, and it kept the sun from heating the water.

A flash of red bounced over the waves. My eyes caught the movement. About a mile away, a kite soared in the air. The surfer holding onto the other end of the rope was nothing but a dot. They were moving fast, though.

I've toyed with the idea of getting some kite surfing gear. The problem is that it's one more thing to store in my already tiny living space. I'd recently given up the idea of adding a kayak. The exercise would be great, but I would lose a sizeable chunk of deck space. I didn't have a garage to store all those fun toys in. So I have to settle for using *Beth* to explore and get my exercise elsewhere.

The red kite grew as the surfer came closer. The wind was coming out of the east at a breezy 15 knots. Kite surfing was similar to sailing, or so I assumed. With 15 knots of wind, I could get *Carina* moving well over 30 knots downwind.

The surfer was tacking back and forth, keeping the kite filled with air. The surfboard would rise off the wave's crest and seem to hang a foot or two above the surface of the water before the surfer landed the jump.

With a fork, I prodded the flesh of the snapper. White meat flaked up as the tines scraped across it, and I scooped the fillet onto an aluminum camping plate.

The kite surfer was now only 500 yards offshore. A distinctly feminine figure rode the board, pointing it toward my beach, perhaps as a temporary resting point.

The woman on the board was wearing a black Neoprene spring suit, a wetsuit with short legs and arms to provide more maneuverability for surfers. A stripe of green sliced through the front of her suit at an angle.

Even from this distance, I could see her smile gleaming as she played over the tops of the waves.

The surfboard rode the curling white foam as it rolled upon the beach. Leaping off the board, she twisted her arms, directing the kite into a nosedive that embedded the peak into the white sand.

As I scooped a forkful of snapper into my mouth, I watched the woman grab the board from the receding surf and anchor it in the sand. There was an awkwardness in the air. I wasn't sure if I was somehow interrupting her, or vice versa. It only took a second to note the brazen fire in her eyes. She didn't care who she disturbed. This was her world–she intended to conquer it.

Not that I minded. Most of my life seems to be in solitude, but I do enjoy the company of people. And a strong, willful woman will pique my interest every time.

Of course, the smart play for me was to enjoy my snapper in peace.

"You got the whole place to yourself?" she shouted over the surf.

"Well, I did."

Her pearly smile spread wide. "I'm interrupting you?"

Returning her smile, I responded, "Not at all. In fact, I just finished cooking lunch if you like snapper."

Her fingers tugged the zipper on her spring suit down to relieve the tension around her neck. "I'd hate to intrude on your solitude."

"I've had enough of the voices in my head, anyway."

"One of mine always speaks in Mandarin," she joked. "He's an annoying shit."

She dropped to the sand beside me. "I'm Rikki," she introduced.

"Chase."

"Are you stranded out here, Chase?"

"Nope, I came out here of my own accord."

As she studied the tattoo on my arm, Rikki asked, "You're a Marine?"

"I was. Once upon a time."

She nodded. There wasn't any more to be said.

"I only have the one plate and fork, though," I stated as I handed her the other fillet of snapper.

"I'm not so classy I can't eat with my fingers." With that, her right index and middle finger dug into the flaky white meat and spooned it into her mouth.

Bits of meat fell onto her chest. A spurt of laughter exploded from her lips, spewing fish unceremoniously.

"I'm sorry," she muttered. "I'm quite the lady."

"You looked good on the kite," I offered. "You are a long way out here."

"Naw, I'm anchored on the other side of that island," she responded, pointing toward a couple of land masses in the distance.

A dot on the water appeared to be another dinghy skating across the water in our direction.

"What about you?" she asked.

My head nodded in the opposite direction as I answered, "I'm anchored about five miles that way. Found a nice little cut in a key with ample holding."

"You just wanted to come camping?"

"I like the stars."

She rolled onto her back and stared up at the clouds drifting by overhead. "You don't get stars on your boat?"

"Maybe I like sand."

Rikki twisted to face me. "No one likes sand. It's the bane of the beach."

"I don't know," I refuted, "I like the feel of it."

She gave me a smile.

The boat in the distance grew closer. Its trajectory seemed to be our island. The area was getting a little more crowded than I wanted. Like Rikki, it was, no doubt, some cruisers out exploring the islands.

Rikki continued to pick at the snapper, trying to catch every tiny flake of meat.

"Are you alone on your boat?" she asked.

"Right now," I commented with a smirk. "How about you? Is there someone waiting for you to come back?"

"Just my husband," she answered. "He will probably be out looking for me. He has quite a jealous bone."

I lifted an eyebrow, and she started laughing.

"No," she amended, "I'm kidding—no husband for me. I can't even handle taking care of a cat. I certainly don't need to be responsible for another human."

My lip curled, and I remarked, "Yeah, cats are the worst."

She gave my arm a playful tug. "You've obviously never had a husband. At least cats shit in a box."

"You speak from experience."

"Just one," she responded. "Lasted eight months, which was seven and half longer than it should have."

The dinghy was closer. It was an inflatable type with a large and loud outboard on the stern.

"You sure that's not your ex?" I asked, pointing at the gray boat beelining toward us.

She glanced out and shook her head. "No, my ex would have to dry out for three days before he could drive that straight of a line."

"I don't think I have enough fish for them too."

She laughed again. It was the sort of laugh that had a lot of practice, but still felt genuine.

"I don't know about them, but I only came because of the fresh fish."

There were two men in the boat. Something about their demeanor told me they weren't sight-seeing.

The bottom of the boat scraped across the sand about 50 feet from where we sat, the outboard motor stalling as the propeller dug into the sand. It became evident as I watched them that they were not regular cruisers. Too many landings like that and that $3000 outboard would become useless.

My initial thought was that they might be some charter customers, spending a few days on a boat. These two sported chiseled physiques, though. Abnormally so. Bodybuilders. The type that has to supplement the hours in the gym with whatever compound creates such obscene cuts of muscle.

Not the type I see out on the water much.

They climbed out of the dinghy, leaving it mired in the sand. Both of them were wearing short-sleeved t-shirts, probably to keep their arms on display.

"You sure you don't know them?" I asked Rikki.

She shook her head as she watched them.

The tattoos on both of them were older, having been inked into their skin before the muscle increase occurred. The newly formed bulges of muscle contorted a couple of the images. One had an eagle or hawk on his forearm. The other a Punisher tattoo. Nothing congruent about the artwork. Except for the distinct lines of a Swastika just above both men's right elbow.

Despite being somewhat obscured by their sleeves, the symbol was a glaring declaration. One that made me tense up. These men were on a mission.

I glanced over at Rikki. She knew what they wanted too.

"Hey guys," I smiled and waved with as much affable generosity as I could muster.

The two men moved toward us in an odd sort of unison. They both wore off-the-rack combat boots, the toes digging into the sand with each step.

The hair on the back of my neck stood on end. My day was about to change directions.

I jumped to my feet when the man on the right pulled a Glock 9 mm out and leveled it at me.

"Just stay down," he ordered.

2

Nothing appears bigger than the barrel of a gun pointed at a person's face. This particular gun was a Glock 34. The magazine could hold at least 17 rounds plus one in the barrel. Fully loaded, it weighed a hair over two pounds. A bullet fired from the barrel will travel up to 1,230 feet per second. Those kinds of details mattered in a moment like this.

Staring up at the man with the gun I calculated his distance from me–over six feet. With a calculator, I could figure out it would take less than 500th of a second for the bullet to leave the barrel and obliterate my skull.

If I was standing already, I might close that gap before he reacted. But, seated and with Rikki between him and me, there was no chance of disarming him. So, think, don't react. Yet.

The only difference between the two men was the color of their eyes. One blue, one brown. Both were decidedly Caucasian. I mean, only a moronic white dude thinks a Swastika tattoo is tasteful artwork. Other than the eye color, they could have been twins. Both had the same hair-style, short with a part on the left side. Their steroid-induced musculature was identical, as if poured from the same mold.

The Aryan twins scowled at us. Brown Eyes pointed the Glock at Rikki.

"Get up," he ordered. His drawl was Southern.

"What do you want?" I demanded.

"Shut up!" Blue Eyes snapped. "Just shut up!"

There's a Southern accent, and then there's a rural Southern accent. The long drawn out way Blue Eyes said the word "shut" indicated a rural Southern dialect. Even having been born and raised in the South, I wasn't able to distinguish what area they might have come from. Tennessee, Alabama, or Georgia.

"No one has to get hurt," Brown Eyes commented in a calm tone, pulling me from my mental analysis of their accents.

Of course, he was wrong. Someone was going to get hurt.

He wanted to control the situation. Keep everyone focused on the promise that no one would be hurt. If he could do that, he could do the job he came to do.

A job was precisely what it felt like. They came on a mission for Rikki. Someone sent them to get her. There was nothing random about their arrival.

The one misfire to their mission–me. They were told Rikki would be alone. Out on her surfboard. Grab her while she was alone, and no one would be the wiser.

They didn't expect me. That meant that improvisation was in order, and these two goons didn't think for themselves.

When they first saw Rikki on shore with someone, they decided that with their combined brawn, two against one seemed like good odds. They were, after all, a force to be reckoned with. Who, in their right minds, would oppose such a force?

By the time they got close enough to recognize that I might be such an opposing force, determination set in. They couldn't confer with each other without showing weakness. Backing off wasn't an option either. Had they been operating independently, stepping back and waiting for Rikki to be alone would be the shrewd play.

Brown Eyes knew they screwed up, too. He was the smarter of the two. Maybe that's why he got the gun.

Now, he was trying to evaluate what to do. The Aryan twins were on a mission, meaning they were just doing what they were told. They would have been simple orders: find the black girl with the kite.

They wanted Rikki, and their actions indicated she needed to be alive and cooperative. The intelligent thing would have been to put a bullet in me right now and take her. Brown Eyes considered that and dismissed it. Her cooperation might diminish if those kinds of stakes became clear.

Blue Eyes, on the other hand, wanted to kill me on sight. I'm glad he wasn't the smarter of the two.

"Get up," Blue Eyes ordered Rikki.

She moved to stand, and I scooted toward the burning coals.

"Rikki," I spoke, enunciating each syllable, "you need to be careful."

"Quiet!" Brown Eyes demanded. Then his voice lowered. "No one is going to get hurt. She is going to come with us, and you get to stay here."

"It's fine," Rikki assured me as she moved toward Blue Eyes.

"Take her back to the boat," Brown Eyes told his twin.

Blue Eyes grabbed Rikki by the arm and walked her toward the dinghy.

"What about him?" Rikki asked, pointing at me.

Brown Eyes glanced at her. "He's going to be fine."

That was a lie. I knew it, and Brown Eyes knew it. But, most importantly, Rikki knew it.

He couldn't leave me here. If Blue Eyes left in the inflatable tender, the only other way off the island was in my dinghy. Which meant that I wouldn't need it.

The lie was his mistake. He had no choice, but he should have tried to mask the deception better.

A line from a movie popped somewhat unceremoniously into my head. "We are men of action. Lies do not become us."

A timer was counting down, and I did not know how long I had. Best guess–as long as it took to get Rikki out of earshot. That would be a very short distance from shore.

Blue Eyes tried to push the dinghy out with one hand. Instead, the mired motor left the inflatable bound on shore. He released his grip on Rikki to jostle the boat out of the sand.

The next few seconds slowed. Rikki took advantage of his distraction. She spun around and drove a heel kick into Blue Eye's knee. The blow sent the Nazi down on that knee.

"Bitch!" he howled over the pounding surf.

Brown Eyes reacted on instinct, turning to see his partner falling into the surf. Scrambling, I grabbed the speargun and rolled as the Aryan realized his error. The gun vibrated as the spear shot toward the gunman.

A flash fired from the Glock. Next to me, sand erupted as the bullet sprayed granules around.

His face turned down with widened eyes at the 20-inch shaft protruding from his chest.

I was on my feet and charging him a split second later. My shoulder drove up into him, picking him up and dropping him into the sand.

The Glock had fallen from his grip. My left hand scooped it up. As I came down to my knee, I moved the gun to my right hand. Blue Eyes was struggling to his feet, unaware of Brown Eye's fate yet. Instead, he focused on Rikki, who was trying to keep the inflatable boat between her and Blue Eyes.

The 9 mm kicked as I fired. Blue Eyes never heard the shot. He jerked and twisted before collapsing into the water.

Brown Eyes wheezed. His fingers wrapped around the spear, trying to pull it out. The effort was futile. He was dead whether or not he pulled it out. From the angle it punctured his chest, the barbs on the end would tear his heart apart when it came out. If it wasn't removed, it would just be a slow death from internal bleeding.

As I crawled to my feet, I considered stopping him as he tugged desperately on the shaft. However, it was a passing thought, and I decided he could make his own choice.

Rikki stared at me. Her pupils were dilated and still. Calmer than I felt.

"Are you okay?" I shouted as she walked back to me.

She nodded as she looked at Brown Eyes, who had successfully pulled the barbed spear out of his chest. His lifeless eyes here stared up.

"What the hell is going on?" I asked her.

She turned her eyes back to me before they shifted over my shoulder. My head turned to follow her gaze. Another inflatable dinghy in the distance was on a direct heading to this island.

"Seriously," I muttered. My eyes locked with Rikki's as I exclaimed, "We need to go!"

My hand grabbed the speargun, and I took a quick look around the campground. The rest of my gear would have to wait for me to come back.

Tethered to a tree, my little dinghy's motor was no match for the 150 horsepower outboard attached to the Aryans' boat. But that motor wasn't going anywhere now until someone took the time to dig it out.

"Come on," I urged as I ran toward *Beth*.

With a flick of my wrist I loosened the painter's hitch and tossed the rope into the front of the dinghy. Rikki grabbed the starboard side with no instruction and helped me push the wooden boat into the water.

"Get in the front," I told her as I pointed the little boat out.

Launching any dinghy from shore is a tricky endeavor. The waves want to push everything ashore and trying to lower a motor and start it between waves can be frustrating. Under the pressure of life and death that stress doesn't ease.

The 10 horsepower outboard hanging off *Beth's* transom was in pristine order. One pull, and the motor coughed to life. My hand twisted the throttle, powering us through the next wave before the propeller dug into the sand.

The bow climbed over the rising surf. When it plunged forward, the outboard whirred futilely as the prop came out of the water. Once we cleared the second wave, the sound of the motor leveled off, and *Beth* picked up speed.

Glancing toward the other boat, I watched as it changed direction to follow us.

3

The little outboard screamed at me. I pushed it harder, stretching its abilities. Most of the use it gets is from puttering around islands and carrying me to new snorkeling spots. High-speed chases weren't a common occurrence.

Behind us, the second inflatable dinghy gained on us. We still had over a mile distance between them and us, but if their outboard rivaled the one the Aryan brothers had, it wouldn't take but a few minutes for them to overtake us.

Mentally, I berated myself. The island offered a better defensive position. Out here in the open water, my only bet is evasion.

The boat's bow pointed toward Bahia Honda Key, one of the larger Keys attached to the mainland by U.S. Highway 1. Part of the Bahia Honda State Park, the island was the closest civilization to us.

Unfortunately, seven miles of open water lay between us and it. The other boat would catch up to us in another two miles.

We needed shelter from the storm, so to speak.

The next best choice was just over a mile west: Little Pine Key. A larger island that, like so many of the Keys, had a population of zero. A relatively unknown and out-of-the-way fishing and birding destination. Little Pine Key didn't make the list of tour stops for the popular charter vessels. One had to have their own transportation to visit it, meaning that it remained isolated.

We wouldn't find any help there, but it was still safer than being attacked at sea.

"What are you doing?" Rikki shouted when I made a complete about face with *Beth*.

My finger aimed toward the mangrove covered island as I responded, "We can't outrun them."

She gave me an assuring nod. That was a lot of trust that she had in me after only knowing me for half an hour. I didn't want to disappoint her, in part because a failure would likely mean I would be chalked up as another boater lost at sea.

Beth pushed hard toward the island. I had a lot of faith in the little boat. She could take a pretty severe beating. The outboard, on the other hand, worried me.

Just make it another half mile, I urged the little engine.

It continued its high-pitched scream in response. Something I took as good. It would deserve a good oil change and tune-up as a reward.

The dinghy closed in on us—enough for me to distinguish two men. From this distance they looked like clones of the other two: blond and brawny.

The mangroves that shrouded the shoreline offered a small opening, doubtless created by local fishermen. The other boat hounded us. I estimated they were less than five minutes behind us. Not a lot of time to land the vessel and find cover.

The gunwales on either side of the wooden tender scraped against the overgrown shrubs. The motor pushed us faster than we should go in such a tight spot. With one hand, I released the throttle, raised the propeller out of the water, and killed the engine. The hull scraped against the rocky bottom before lurching to a stop.

"Go!" I urged Rikki, who was already scurrying over the bow.

With the Glock nestled under my waistband, I wasn't going to be able to run like that, though. The designer of my swimsuit never intended for it to holster weapons. My hand pulled the Glock free, and I jumped clear of the dinghy.

My feet splashed into the water.

"Damn," I screeched when my bare feet dug into the chunks of limestone. Then, I remembered my sandals, still nestled together next to my hammock.

Rikki vanished into the brush. The second boat pushed through the edge of the mangroves. I grabbed the speargun off the bottom of the watercraft before following Rikki into the overgrowth.

Most of the islands have very little old growth. A few palm trees sprout up and survive. Most of the vegetation only rises about six to eight feet. For guerrilla warfare, it's ideal. Lots of cover.

Rikki ran a few strides ahead of me. She moved with laser-like intensity. Calm and clear-headed. Maybe more than me. She might not be accustomed to this type of life-threatening excitement, but she was obviously not a stranger to it.

We got just over a hundred feet from the shore when I stopped Rikki.

"Here," I offered her the 9 mm. "You keep moving. Stay down and avoid them. I want to see if we can split them up."

Her fingers wrapped around the grip of the Glock. For a split second, we locked eyes. Her amber eyes burned. She blinked and sprinted away.

Through the greenery, the outboard of the second boat sounded like it slowed. A second later, silence.

On my hands and knees through the thickest growth I could find, I pulled the band on the speargun back to cock it and waited. It made sense that at least one of these two also had a gun, if not both.

I wanted to think it was my skill that let me impale Brown Eyes, that my spearfishing abilities were near expert. But truthfully, luck played a heavy hand. And a little twist of ignorant confidence. Sometimes being too stupid to realize that something might not work—allows luck to double down.

Thing One and Two came barreling through the mangroves like bull elephants. Both of them held guns at the ready. Another 9 mm Glock and a Sig Sauer P320. My breathing stopped as I watched from ten feet away. One speargun wasn't going to cut it.

Both men wore black short-sleeved muscle shirts. The blue-gray ink of the SS tattoos was clearly visible on both of their right arms.

"Which way?" Thing One grunted. Maybe he was Thing Two. I couldn't tell who had the lead.

"Go that way," the second ordered. "I'll circle over there. They can't go far."

"Where are Jacob and Rich?" Thing Two asked aloud.

"I don't fucking know!" Thing One snapped. "Just go that way."

"What about the guy with her?"

"We leave him to feed the gators," Thing One snarled.

Thing Two traipsed toward the western side of the island. The other tried to follow the eastern coast. Rikki had cut straight through the brush. These two made enough noise, trampling around that she should be able to avoid them for days.

Of course, I didn't want to be playing hide and seek with Nazis for days. To be honest, I didn't want to do anything with the Nazis.

After he passed, I crawled to my feet. Thing Two crept through the brush 30 yards ahead of me. I lost track of Thing One when he got far enough away.

Crouching, I weaved through the brush. The limestone rocks crunched under my feet. A stealthy approach seemed unlikely.

Flanking him would be the best option, but it also meant I might run into his partner. Better to bring him back to me.

With my head down and my face aimed at the ground, I let out a loud grunt. The kind of sound one might make trying to climb around. The island carried the sound through the underbrush.

The Nazi's feet froze. From my hiding place in the mangroves, I could just make out the green boots turning slowly as he tried to pinpoint the location of the noise. I imagined his head cocked in different directions as he tried to hear anything over the wind and waves.

The timbre of my voice dropped as I let out a softer grunt. The boots crunched toward me.

The speargun stretched out in front of me like a sniper rifle. He had to be close. Too close for comfort, but my options were limited.

His feet shuffled a few paces, paused, and shuffled some more. Finally, he came to a stop within ten feet of me. He couldn't see me, and I could only see his calves and feet.

Ninety percent of the world is right-handed. If he fell in that group, he would step forward with his right foot. I held my breath and waited. He finally took a step toward me.

The speargun let out a thrum as the rubber band released its tension. The spear struck Thing Two's shin, just below his knee. The shaft glanced off the tibia and skittered across the limestone rocks.

The force of the spear still buckled the Nazi's knee, and he howled in pain as he dropped. He let go of the Sig in his hand to catch a branch before he hit the ground.

Flying up out of the brush, I lifted the pistol grip of the speargun and drove it into his surprised face. The first blow knocked him back. As he fell to the ground, I followed through with two more fast thrusts. The man's head lolled to the side; blood smeared across his face.

His chest was rising with each breath, but he couldn't go anywhere soon.

The Sig P320 fit into my hand. A quick check confirmed it was fully loaded.

I breathed a sigh of relief. Amateurs, but even amateurs have an advantage over an unarmed opponent.

The unconscious Aryan lay slumped on the ground. I decided to leave him. He'd wake up, eventually. For now, he couldn't do anything.

Rikki was still in danger, and Thing One might prove a bit more dangerous than his brother. He had a lead on me, so I hurried down the path he took.

Little Pine Key boasted a larger area than some of the other islands. We landed on the narrow southern tip. Rikki had a head start, but I thought that I could make up for that time. I needed to get in front of her and Thing One before they reached the middle of the island. There would be a couple of square miles to search, making this game of hide and seek stretch out.

My bare feet slowed me down across the rocky terrain, but I figured I was still making better time than Thing One. Then. it occurred to me that I wasn't sure if Rikki was wearing shoes. I tried to remember if she had some sort of water sock on her feet when she got off the surfboard, but her feet were the last thing I noticed.

After several minutes, I decided to cut east and intercept Rikki or her pursuer.

Two gunshots echoed across the island. My head lowered as I pushed through the brush in the direction of the gunfire. The initial shots sounded southeast of me. I guessed around 50 to 100 yards away. The echoes made it hard to distinguish.

Rikki held the Glock 34 in her outstretched hand. Thing One stared at the blue skies, unblinking. Two round holes tore through his muscle shirt. His dark blood mixed with the black cloth.

She whipped the barrel around as I came through the mangroves. She held her fire when she saw me. A second later, she relaxed.

"You good?" I asked.

"Yeah," she confirmed. "What about the other one?"

"He's down, but still alive," I answered, waving the gun like a trophy. "Best he'll do is limp out."

"Did you see any more of them?"

I shook my head. "Come on," I prodded, "let's get out of here."

We hiked back to *Beth*. Rikki didn't seem fazed after killing Thing One. She possessed a stoic facade. The woman bouncing across the waves earlier was hiding, but she'd be back. Right now, Rikki had switched to battle mode, something I had experienced many times. An hour from now, the smiling, happy face would come back, letting this Rikki rest.

The same could be said of my dark side. Killing wasn't fun, required at times, but never fun. The moment I experienced any glee from killing anyone, even Nazis, I would know I've gone too far. I'm not sure that there is a way to come back from that. So, for now, I try to breathe in, breathe out, and move on.

The Things' inflatable dinghy pressed up against *Beth's* stern. I waded out, pushing it free of the mangroves. After firing three rounds into the PVC sides, I watched the air escape the tubes. A few seconds later, I climbed in *Beth* and got the little outboard motor purring. I would remember the maintenance I silently promised her earlier.

4

The motor died as I flipped the kill switch. *Beth* slowed to a drift two miles from Little Pine Key. Despite the calm water, the little wooden boat pitched along with the waves.

"What are you doing?" Rikki asked from the bow of the boat.

"I want to know why three people are dead? What have you gotten into? Who's after you?"

She shook her head. "I haven't got a clue who they were," she insisted.

My eyebrow lifted as I responded, "This wasn't random. You were the target."

She didn't answer.

"Nazis!" I pointed out, my voice escalating an octave. "Why are Nazis after you?"

"I think they are more like Neo-Nazis," she corrected.

Scowling, I stated with blunt efficacy, "Still a Nazi."

She nodded.

"I'd just like a little explanation, Rikki."

"I don't know who they are," she responded at last. "But I might have an idea what they want."

She paused. "I'm something of a historian," she explained. "Over the last few months, I've been doing some research on a Nazi plot to kidnap the Duke of Windsor back in 1940."

"That was over 80 years ago. They seem a little sore still."

"Look, Chase, I'm sorry. I don't understand it," she pleaded. "That's the only connection I have to anything related to Nazis."

"The Duke of Windsor?" I questioned.

"Yes, Edward. He abdicated the throne in 1936 to marry an American divorcee. He was also a suspected Nazi sympathizer. Under that premise, the German government concocted a plot to kidnap him and use his influence against England. Some theorize that Hitler intended to give him back the throne after Germany was victorious."

My elbows rested on my knees, and I leaned toward her. "I don't understand. This is historical, right? So, why would anyone want to kidnap you for it?"

She offered a shrug, and I felt my face twist with skepticism.

"We need to find a radio and contact the authorities."

Her countenance soured. "Do we want to get dragged into it?"

"Rikki, there are two dead bodies lying next to my camp. Not to mention, my speargun, which killed one of them, is lying in the mangroves back there, along with another corpse. All the cops need is one fingerprint to prove I was there. I'd rather be the one controlling the narrative than having to explain it after the fact."

She sighed. Too much wasn't being said. More than I felt comfortable with. Take her back to her boat, call the Monroe County Sheriff's Department, and wash my hands of the whole thing. That's the smart play.

"Where is your boat anchored?"

Without thinking, she pointed east, saying, "A few miles that way."

The little outboard fired to life with one pull. I adjusted our heading and turned the bow of *Beth* west and twisted the throttle.

Rikki turned her body to face forward. We rode in silence for twenty minutes. The woman was hiding something from me. For a good reason, I supposed. She hadn't known me for more than three hours. I didn't trust her either.

A small island, only 200 feet wide, rose a few feet above sea level, making it barely visible on the horizon. The top deck of a large yacht loomed on the opposite side of the little key. *Beth* skirted around the northern point of the small rocky outcrop.

The vessel in front of me measured at least 60 feet long. She sported at least three decks rising above the hull, and I guessed another two below deck.

Rikki stared at the yacht as we approached. I studied her with intent.

A historian, she said. I chose the wrong field if that's what historians are using for research. No snap judgments, Chase, I scolded myself. Another layer peeled away from Rikki.

Her head stayed focused on the white boat. Again, a defiant refusal to glance back at me. She guessed I made certain assumptions about her.

A multi-million dollar yacht always brings people to draw conclusions. Every marina I have visited had that trait. A new luxury yacht pulls in, and every denizen is speculating: Is it a movie star? Tech mogul? It's unjust speculation. The same type of bias that anyone shows when they learn I live on a sailboat. That must be nice. How do you afford that?

"What is she?" I asked over the din of the outboard.

"A Nomad SUV," she responded.

I wasn't familiar with the name. I smiled and told her, "She's a beaut."

Rikki bowed her head.

"What's her name?"

"*Talitha*."

The stern of *Talitha* sported a hydraulic door that lowered to create a sea-level platform and open up a garage for tenders. A wooden Chris Craft runabout sat on a lift inside the garage.

The motor slowed as I pulled up along the stern until we gently bumped against the boat. Rikki climbed out and lashed the painter to a cleat that she raised from the platform. I secured the stern to a similar cleat.

Rikki stood on the platform and stared up at the structure above us.

"What's wrong?" I asked.

"I'm not sure," she muttered. "Where's Sam?"

"Sam?"

"He's my steward. He or Captain Carlson should have come out."

Rikki moved toward the narrow steps leading up to the next deck.

My right hand caught her arm. "Wait," I ordered.

Her head pivoted to look at me.

"Those guys found you while out on the water," I pointed out.

Her nostrils flared as she inhaled, and her eyes turned to look up toward the bridge.

The two guns we took off the would-be kidnappers remained hidden under the front seat of the dinghy. My foot stepped back into the tender as I retrieved them, handing the Glock back to Rikki.

"We need to take it slow," I told her. "Clear each deck."

"You think someone might still be here?"

"I'm thinking that someone told them where to find you."

Anger flared up in her face. A second passed, and I watched her calm herself in a slow, deep breath. Her wrist rotated the Glock as she judged the weight of the weapon in her hand, before motioning me to lead the way.

The Sig Sauer aimed up the stairwell as I crept up each step. Outdoor chairs and a couch formed a circle around a propane fire-pit. The deck was empty. Behind the sofa, a small bar stood under the deck. A sliding glass door beside the bar was ajar.

With my left hand, I slid the door open. The galley spread out in front of me. Four burners, a double oven, and a full-sized refrigerator spawned a streak of envy through me. *Carina's* galley comprised of a two-burner alcohol stove that seemed to only allow me to use one burner at a time, an oven that could only fit half a frozen pizza, and a dorm-sized fridge. The full-size fridge clinched it for me. Oh, the cold beer I could store in that beast.

An open salon spread out past the galley. A 55-inch television hung on the wall. A leather sectional twisted around. Cup holders molded into the arm rests. A little envy burned inside me.

Rikki moved behind me. A closed door stood on the starboard side of the room.

Pointing at the door, I mouthed, "What's there?"

"Cabins," she mouthed.

"Wait," I whispered as I opened the door. Four steps descended to a corridor. From a tactical standpoint, a hallway can be a terrible place to be. One might as well be in a shooting gallery, from either direction. Three cabin doors lined the two walls: two on the port and one forward. Any of those rooms could provide a protected shooting blind.

Groaning, I decided to risk it. Those cabins needed to be checked.

Stay here, I motioned to Rikki.

With slow steps, I cut my eyes from door to door, searching for the slightest movement. My leg muscles adjusted without thought, shifting the weight of my body from one to the other as the deck swayed with the waves.

The movement registered low on the discomfort meter, nothing like the sloshing *Carina* might receive.

All the cabin doors swung inward. Each had a small latch with enough resistance to keep the doors secured while in rougher seas.

The bottom of the Sig's grip rested on my left forearm as my hand twisted the catch. The door opened to reveal an empty cabin. I moved to the next two doors to find only empty cabins.

Rikki paced a small path in front of the door when I came out of the corridor.

"Nothing," I whispered.

The first sign of any concern crossed her face. She worried about the crew. Until now, she seemed unfazed by the attacks on us. Now worry covered her demeanor.

"Let's go up," I suggested, pointing the barrel at another set of stairs that ascended to the next deck.

The sooner we made sure that no hostiles were aboard, the sooner we could determine the status of her crew.

When my head raised over the three-foot wall at the top of the stairs, I froze.

A man was sprawled on the floor. Nothing distinguishable on him. Blood covered his face, which had taken a beating until his cheekbones turned to pulp. One of his eyes appeared to be ruptured.

Rikki's tension emanated from her. She must have sensed something. Her hand grabbed the back of my shorts as if silently asking me what I saw.

My head turned toward her. "Come on," I told her.

"Sam!" she exclaimed, rushing past me.

She dropped the Glock on the floor as she slid to her knees next to the man and lifted him up. Blood sputtered from his lips and nose.

"He's breathing!" She looked up at me. "We need to get him help!"

"I'm heading to the bridge," I told her. "Stay with him."

As soon as I saw Sam was alive, I wasn't worried about finding any opposition on board. They got what they needed out of Sam and left him to die. The fact he hadn't died surprised me. I've seen men succumb from a hell of a lot less. Sam wasn't a big man. In fact, he was skinny. While I couldn't tell his age, I felt that he was older, at least in his 60s. Not someone that has the stamina to hold up under that kind of abuse.

He was lying in the middle of a dining room. The table and six chairs lay on their side. Sam's face left a bloody imprint on the edge of the table. One chair splintered into pieces, and I guessed one of the Nazis used it on the lithe little steward.

Another set of steps led up to the bridge. The captain's body slumped against the rear wall. The front of his white starched uniform was brown with dried blood. His lifeless head lolled to the side.

I stared at the Sig Sauer in my hand, wondering if it was the one that killed Rikki's captain.

5

Moses Carter stared down at me with a 12 gauge sawed-off shotgun resting on his shoulder. It wasn't actually Moses Carter. The poster looked like it might have been one that hung in a theater marquee in 1983.

I wish I could say that my movie trivia game was strong enough to know the film's actual release date despite coming out several years before I was born. No, the copyright date was my cue. I didn't recall ever seeing the film. I recognized the actor, but the movie poster provided his name, in case it escaped me. In bold letters it read, "Benjamin Dexter is Moses Carter."

Isolated in the lounge area next to the galley, I stretched my feet out and took in the decor. It was a trophy room. Several placards and movie posters adorned the walls. *Rise Up Moses* was the most prominent picture of the collection.

His eyes, staring down from the wall at me, were very familiar. Those same eyes are the ones I saw a few hours ago on an isolated beach.

When the first officers arrived on the scene, they separated us after they confiscated our weapons. Within minutes, the beating blades of an evac chopper bore down on us.

Sam was still breathing when the officers arrived, a feat that seemed miraculous. Every second that passed pushed him closer to the edge. The first officer named Koplin, according to his nameplate, wasted no time in assessing the situation. The steward was going to die if he didn't get him treated, and the fastest way to get him to a hospital was an air evac. Tricky work when there's no place to land.

The din of the rotating blades echoed through the boat. When I glanced out earlier, the crew lowered a gurney while the pilot held the helicopter steady.

An officer stood sentry in the galley, making sure that I didn't make a run for it. I wasn't about to make a fuss. The attention needed to be on getting Sam off the vessel alive. Time made little difference in the military. Life was a constant state of "wait and see."

So, I'm killing time by staring at 80s action memorabilia. At least there wasn't a screen playing loops of Benjamin Dexter's greatest hits. My bare feet rested on a glass coffee table, and I reclined on the settee.

Besides the constant hurry-up-and-wait attitude that the Marines instilled in me, there was also the ability to close my eyes and drop asleep in any circumstance. The adrenaline crash left me a little tired, and I let my mind work over the last couple of hours while I drifted into a cat nap.

"Mr. Gordon," a voice woke me up.

My eyes opened in a flutter, trying to adjust to the light. I realized I'd been asleep for a few minutes. The boat was silent, and I guessed the helicopter came and left with Sam.

A thin white-haired man stood on the other side of the coffee table. He wore shorts and a tan short-sleeved polo shirt. A .45 Beretta hung in a holster on his right hip. He appeared to be in his 50s. A jagged scar ran along his calf. The pattern was familiar, the kind of scar left after a piece of metal is removed.

My feet dragged off the table as I sat up. He stared at the tattoo on my shoulder.

"Marine?" he asked.

"Yeah," I responded. "Not anymore."

He pulled up his sleeve. The ink faded with the years, but the "U.S.M.C." was still visible. "Been awhile, but..." he trailed off.

I nodded. We were silent for a full second. He was trying to make some immediate connection through experiences shared decades apart. We had the same brothers that we never met.

It was, of course, bullshit.

He already talked to Rikki. The procedure made sense. This was her yacht, and the crew worked for her. I was still an outlier. The first responders already had my name, which meant that Cooper had already had the chance to run me through all the alphabet specific databases.

Which meant that he knew I was a Marine long before he spotted my tattoo. He was playing the brother veteran. He wanted me to feel like he was on my side.

The problem he was trying to understand was me. Where did I come from? How did I end up saving Rikki? What was in it for me?

I was the random stranger that needed to be explained. A coincidence. Cops don't like coincidences. Hell, I don't either. They are too rare and unpredictable to explain.

Which puts me as the number one person of interest in this affair. Pieces of the puzzle had to fit together to make sense. Cooper was already running scenarios through his head.

I could almost hear his thoughts. Did I set the whole thing up? Is there a better way to ingratiate oneself into a wealthy woman's life than save her from a harrowing life and death experience?

I was already running explanations through my head. Rikki wasn't telling me the whole truth. Was this some attempted kidnapping? Benjamin Dexter might pay a lot of that Moses Carter money to get his daughter back. If that was the case, then why the crap about being a historian?

"I'm Detective Eric Cooper," he introduced.

I said nothing, just offered a nod.

"We found a couple of bodies over on Little Sonesta Key."

I made no movement to agree or confirm anything, just listened. His people would have found my gear and suspect I had been there.

"Would you care to tell me what you killed the first one with?" He showed me his phone. Brown Eyes filled the screen; the sand coated the wound in his chest, mixing with the dried blood.

One thing I've learned. Lying will never get you far with the police. I might not like to give all the information, but lying is hard to come back from. I only do that in extreme circumstances. This wasn't one of those times. Anything I said would be honest.

"Speargun," I told him.

"Speargun?" he asked. "That's a hell of a shot."

I shrugged. "I had a lot of incentive."

He lifted an eyebrow. "Where's the speargun?"

"I dropped it on Little Pine."

"When you upgraded to the Sig?" he asked.

"Although the guy I took the Sig from was still alive. He might have a little limp and a big lump on his head, but he was alive."

"But you killed the other three?"

"No," I corrected him. "Just two. It was very much a them-or-me sort of situation."

Cooper sat down on the couch. "Tell me what happened from the start."

Without going into details, I gave Cooper the "mission report." If he didn't ask, I didn't expound.

"You never met Ms. Talen before today?" Cooper asked.

"No," I answered. "The first time I saw her was on Little Sonesta."

Cooper cocked his head and studied me. When he seemed to have memorized my face, he let his eyes sweep over the posters and lobby cards hanging around the lounge.

"Are you a fan of Benjamin Dexter?" he asked.

"He's a little ahead of my time," I pointed out.

Cooper gave a brief nod. "I remember a few from my childhood."

"Until your officer quarantined me in here," I offered, "I did not know that Rikki was his daughter."

He appraised me for a second. Finally, he asked, "Where do you live?"

"My boat, which is anchored a few miles away," I answered, "but my permanent address would be in West Palm Beach. My home marina is the Tilly Marina."

"What's your contact information?" he asked.

"You have to call the Manta Club at The Tilly. They hold all my messages."

"Cell phone?" he inquired.

"I don't have one."

His eyes narrowed.

"No Sat phone either."

He crossed his legs. "I don't suppose you have an email."

"Of course, I do," I smiled. "I don't have a computer though, so I don't check it often."

"Let me understand this," he started. "You don't have any means of contact? That's pretty odd, don't you think?"

"I don't know, Detective," I explained. "I find it incredibly freeing. There isn't anyone that I know that needs to reach me on the spur of the moment."

"What about family?" I couldn't tell how much of his questions were simple curiosity or something more sinister. Most people don't hide away from everybody. They can't. Or rather, they convince themselves it's impossible.

"I don't like them enough to worry about it," I explained. "If they could contact me, then it would be a constant barrage of either begging or berating. Neither of which I care for. Not enough to pay an extra bill to endure."

Cooper pursed his lips. It intrigued him. It's a typical response. Most people think about cutting people off, and when they hear me talk about it, they consider, at least for a split second, what their life would be like if they did the same.

"How about you make your way to a marina and call me so I know where I can reach you?" he suggested.

The corner of my mouth lifted. "I don't think so. If you want to keep track of me, then you'll need to hold me. I'll, of course, get a lawyer who will point out that you will need to charge me or let me go. Either way, my cooperation will end with that."

The detective scowled. "I thought you were going to be smarter than that. You know, do the honorable thing."

"Don't try and bullshit me, Cooper. You can't slide in here and wave the 'Hey, I'm Corps too,' and think I'm going to roll over. You've been out too damned long if you think that dog will hunt."

"I killed two men in self-defense. There is an eyewitness that will corroborate that. You can hold me for...what? 48 hours. I've done harder time than that."

He gazed at me, weighing his options. Scare tactics weren't working.

"Why don't you contact me, Detective Cooper?" Rikki suggested as she came down the steps. "That way Chase doesn't have to spend a couple of nights in jail, and you'll feel more comfortable about him not running off."

He glanced up at her. "Is he planning to stay with you?"

It was my turn to cut my eyes toward her. Is she suggesting I stay with her?

Pull your head out of your ass, I scolded myself. She might only want you around as a buffer against another attack.

She looked at me with questioning eyes.

"Yeah," I answered, "she's going to need some help moving the boat into the harbor."

"You won't be able to stay on board," Cooper pointed out. "This is still an active crime scene."

"What do you expect me to do?" Rikki asked.

He glanced at me. "My suggestion would be to find a place on shore to stay. One of my guys can give you some names of places."

Annoyed, Rikki folded her arms and stated, "No, we'll be at the Casa Marina."

"Fine," Cooper resigned. "Ms. Talen, I'll be in touch. I expect there will be more questions, please don't leave the area without my consent."

I couldn't help cutting my eyes at the detective. Prudence suggested I hold my tongue despite the urge to explain all the reasons that I don't take orders anymore. I knew I'd prodded the bear enough.

Cooper turned as he was leaving. "I'll let you gather a few items, but then you need to disembark."

Rikki relaxed as soon as he left the lounge.

I turned to her. "Go get some things so we can head to shore. We have a lot of things to talk about."

6

"Let me get us a couple of rooms," Rikki offered when we arrived at the Casa Marina Resort. "Then, we can get you some clothes."

The nonchalance she exhibited in that statement was the first sign that the woman had means. The multi-million dollar yacht was, of course, the clincher. But even being on board the opulent vessel, the aura that Rikki put off wasn't some spoiled rich kid.

She had a sort of humbled arrogance. The lineage of a Hollywood mogul would not be her identity.

From the moment I saw her on the kite board, she was bold and collected. She could fight, and there were no qualms about shooting someone that intended her harm. She was aware of her capability beyond her bank account.

While my beach attire wasn't unusual in any part of Key West, I was going to need to at least acquire a pair of shoes. The flip-flops I borrowed from Rikki were bigger than her kite board, and I was struggling to keep them from slipping off. Despite that, I wanted some answers first.

My hand caught her arm. "Not yet," I insisted. I aimed her toward a sofa in the bar, stating, "I want a conversation."

The deputies hurried us off *Talitha*, and the dinghy ride ashore didn't offer an ideal setting for this discussion.

She rolled her eyes, but offered resignation in one huffed word, "Fine."

Her luggage consisted of a worn Navy seabag. The woman had stuffed whatever she needed for a few days into the canvas bag in less than three minutes. The green duffel dropped to the floor next to a sofa, and Rikki followed suit.

A dark-skinned waitress carrying a serving tray appeared. She placed a ramekin of nuts and two beverage napkins on the table in front of the couch.

"Gin and tonic," Rikki ordered. "Hayman's if you have it. Hendrick's if you don't."

The girl nodded and looked at me.

"Rum and whatever fresh juice you have. I'm not picky."

"You struck me as a beer-only type of guy," Rikki commented.

I ignored her statement and demanded, "I want the truth."

Rikki sat stoically for a second.

"I get it," I suggested. "We just met each other, but three people have died since you dropped off that kite board. Two by my own hands, so I deserve to understand what the hell is going on."

"You're right," she conceded. "I can't thank you enough. In fact, I'm so sorry. I haven't even taken the time to thank you at all."

"Your gratitude can be shown with a little honesty."

She began, "I didn't actually lie to you. I have no idea who these guys are, but what I told you was true. I am looking for a lost shipment of gold that the Nazis lost somewhere in the Bahamas."

"You're a treasure hunter, then?"

Most of the treasure hunters I had met were older men that longed for some adventure. They read one too many H. Rider Haggard books or saw *Romancing the Stone* one too many times. The few that are able to find anything often sell it for far too little and blow the proceeds on their next adventure.

The misconception that somehow finding lost treasure meant unimaginable riches was just folly. Most wrecks that are shallow are no longer lost, and their bounty picked over. Even more problematic were the laws regarding antiquities. The only way to make actual money is to melt it down and sell the gold by the ounce, besides the legal ramifications, that might mean a cultural or historical loss.

"Yes," she answered, "and I can tell what is going through your mind?"

My back leaned against the couch as I smiled. "I am not even sure what that is."

"Yeah, you do. Why is a rich girl like me wanting to do something like running around on a treasure hunt?"

"Everyone has to do something," I pointed out.

"Just so you know, I donate all the treasure. If I can find this gold, then I'll be giving it to the Foundation of Justice. Of course, they'll end up loaning it to a museum, but the point will be that the Nazis will be funding the Foundation's work in fighting to end hate crimes."

"Do you always hunt Nazi gold?"

Rikki shook her head. "No. I've found a few Aztec artifacts and even a box of Spanish doubloons."

"I'm guessing altruism is a side benefit, right?"

She glared at me.

"Come on, Rikki," I explained. "You do it because you love it. I saw you today. Most people would have panicked, but you... You never seemed to flinch."

"Neither did you," she observed.

"No, but I had years of training to handle those type of situations. It wasn't my first time to kill someone, and while I don't regret my actions, the fact is, it carries a hell of a toll."

She nodded. "I guess you noticed the shrine to Benjamin Dexter on *Talitha*."

"Oh," I joked. "Was there something about him there?"

"He's my father. The boat is technically his. It's not the way I would have decorated."

"It seemed somewhat ostentatious," I agreed.

"I was the late-in-life child," she told me. "My mother was an extra he met filming an episode of *Miami Vice*. She died when I was seven years old. He took custody of me."

"I make it sound bad," she continued. "He was a fine dad. Always busy, but he loved me. I just wasn't quite what he expected out of a daughter."

"I wouldn't have a clue what to expect from a daughter," I commented.

"Most of the girls where I attended high school were daughters of the rich and famous. The spoiled girls driving Daddy's Porsche. That wasn't me. I didn't fit in, which in Beverly Hills meant I had to fight to stay afloat. I guess that carried over to adulthood."

"Fine, you're on your own path," I conceded. "On the hunt for Nazi gold. What brought you after this treasure?"

"Last year, I was doing some research in Spain. I found a letter from one of Ramón Grau's supporters, Raul Lopez, to Juan Beigbeder..."

"Whoa." I raised a hand. "I'm pretty much only fluent in American history. I'm going to need some background here."

"Grau was president of Cuba in the 1930s but lost the election. Lopez was a politician that backed his efforts, and Beigbeder was a leader under the Spanish dictator, Franco."

I nodded my understanding, letting her continue.

"The letter was the suggestion that if Germany assisted Grau in taking control of Cuba back, Germany could use Cuba to establish a base in the Gulf of Mexico."

"Okay, that's something scary," I commented.

"No shit," she replied. "Cuba sits only 90 miles from the U.S., and it could easily act as a sentry to almost any access to the Gulf of Mexico. The SS attempted to slip submarines as far as Louisiana on several occasions. With a base as close as Cuba, they could have made more advancements."

"I'm guessing that they did not make such a deal."

"Not entirely," she corrected. "There's no evidence that a deal happened, however, there is a story that circulates around Nassau about a battle between four or five German soldiers and some Americans. This coincided with German plans to kidnap the Duke of Windsor, the appointed governor of the Bahamas. There's no record of an actual fight. The Brits might have cleaned it up to hide the fact that the former king of England had almost joined the Nazis. They get funny about that kind of thing."

"But there are still stories passed down. This was only about 80 years ago, and those stories became legends. Some of which showed that there were more Germans that escaped."

My eyebrow lifted, and I leaned forward, asking, "How did you connect this incident to a coalition with Grau?"

The waitress returned with two drinks. Rikki handed her a credit card.

"More letters," she continued after the waitress moved to another customer. "Beigbeder's correspondence included a telegram from a Nazi Foreign Minister. It referenced Operation Willi, the attempted kidnapping of the duke, as being an opportunity to... basically, it was the German rendition of 'two birds with one stone.' He followed it up with a comment that payment was en route."

"They intended to do what then?" I asked, as I took a sip of my drink. The orange juice was fresh, squeezed in the last five minutes.

"Like I said, German forces patrolled America's coast-line. There's a U-boat sitting at the bottom of the

Gulf, just 130 miles from New Orleans. It would make sense if Germans wanted to slip into the Bahamas; they would do so in a sub. Since the Nazis never established a presence in Cuba, the plan obviously didn't succeed. Perhaps the sub sank somewhere in the Bahamas."

I looked at her with curiosity. "Most of the water around the Bahamas is pretty shallow. So I'd imagine it would have been discovered by now."

"Most, but not all."

"Yeah, the part that's deep is real damn deep."

"Doesn't mean it's not there."

My brow furrowed. "That might be the most illogical thing I have ever heard."

Rikki shrugged. "Quite honestly, I was sure I hit a brick wall. It was a stretch. Until the Nazis showed up."

"You have had no dealings with them before?"

She shook her head. "Nothing."

"What was the last thing you did?" I asked, adding, "As far as your hunt is going."

"I might have found a survivor. A police blotter noted a fisherman brought a man to shore named Henry Richman on January 3, 1941. The man vanished before the police showed up. The fisherman noted that the man had a German accent, and the man's nine-year-old son said the man had the name Vogel on his shirt. It seemed the police searched for him, suspecting he might have been a German spy."

"How much digging did you do on this?"

She laughed. "A lot. It's like the world's biggest puzzle. Sometimes I don't even recognize when I have a piece."

"Where did you find the police blotter?"

"Here at the county records. I was searching for any records of rescues at sea, hoping that maybe someone saw something. A user on a forum about sea stories suggested I check it out. Once I had a clue where to look, it only took a week of digging through papers to find the report."

"When was that?"

"Last Thursday."

"Once you found the blotter, what did you do?"

"Spent hours in the library, looking through the censuses from 1950. If I could find a Richman in those records, I would have a lead."

With the last swallow of my drink, I looked at her. "We need to go back and look at those records then."

"Why?" she asked.

"That seems to be where you shook the tree," I pointed out. "It might be nice to see which branch dropped the fruit on you."

She smiled at me. The taste of the hunt was on her lips. "Good, let's go."

I stopped her with a gesture. "I'd like a shower and a hot meal first."

7

A pink Jeep was the last thing I was expecting when Rikki called my room the next morning to tell me she was downstairs, but it seemed to fit her to a tee. With the breeze blowing through our hair, we ventured toward the county courthouse.

Rikki had taken me and her credit card last night to several clothing stores. I felt a bit like a Ken doll as she dressed me in typical island gear: Tommy Bahama button-down shirt, linen pants, and a pair of Sperry's. At least, I didn't need socks with the shoes. I stopped her at the linen jacket. The next thing would be a tie, and I knew that wouldn't fly.

Key West has a uniqueness to it. The tourists clog the streets, walking from Duval Street toward Sloppy Joe's, Hog's Breath, or whatever saloon they wanted to get their selfies and shots. Once one gets clear of the shopping district, the colorful characters show up. The bright paint and intricate architecture draw my eyes every time. No matter how long I live in South Florida, the Arkansas boy in me is in awe at the sights.

The Monroe County Courthouse is on Fleming Street. Compared to Duvall and Whitehead, the streets around the courthouse are practically empty. As a result, out-of-towners avoid the bureaucracy of paradise.

The Records Department was small. A wiry woman in her 50s sat at the window.

"Oh, you're back," she greeted Rikki. "Did you need to dig around some more?"

"It's possible," she responded to the woman.

"Ma'am," I interrupted, "did anyone express any interest in what she was looking into?"

The lady stiffened. I might as well belch in her face. She took offense.

"What do you mean?"

"Did anyone pass through and ask what she was up to?" I rephrased.

"Oh, why would anyone do that?"

"We aren't sure," I insisted. "Do you remember anyone asking?"

She grunted, "No."

"How many people can access these records?"

"Oh, I wouldn't know that." Her demeanor took a complete turn. She didn't plan to tell us anything.

Rikki glanced at me. I asked her, "Did you sign in here?"

She nodded, and I looked back at the woman behind the desk. "Did anyone come look at the sign-in sheet?"

"I don't watch the sheet."

"Isn't that your job?" I questioned.

"My job is to make sure that people sign in, not to see who looks at the list."

My hand caught Rikki by the arm, and I turned her toward the exit. "Let's go," I suggested. "She doesn't want to help us."

"We certainly overstayed our welcome," Rikki stated in a clear voice.

"What the hell?" she asked when we stepped outside.

"I'm not sure," I admitted. "She might just be offended in general. It's a perpetual habit for some people. Although, she may not want to get in trouble."

Her eyes rolled when she offered, "The other possibility is she just doesn't like black bitches."

I shrugged. "The sign-in sheet might be the thread to you. What made them even get worried? I can only figure that you were on to something."

We stood on the sidewalk. The buildings blocked the breeze, and the subtropical sun was heating us up.

"Did you find anything in the censuses?" I queried.

She shook her head. "No, there weren't any Vogels on the 1950s census in Monroe County. Of course, there are plenty throughout the States, but no idea where I would even start."

"That's almost a decade later though," I pointed out. "He had plenty of time to move anywhere. Changed his name. Back in those days, he might have tried to become less German. I'm sure that wasn't a popular nationality after the war."

Pausing, I let my mind twist around that idea for a second. Finally, I suggested, "Changing your name back then wasn't hard. No computers to cross reference anything. Suppose he just decided becoming red, white, and blue was better than facing confinement as a spy."

Rikki shrugged.

"Did you make a copy of the police report?"

"It's on my iPad."

"Was the fisherman's name on it?"

She nodded.

"If the kid on the boat was 12 in 1940, then he could still be around. He'd be in his 90's."

Rikki walked to a concrete bench and pulled her tablet from the bag slung over her shoulder. While she navigated her iPad, I studied the street. Even in the non-touristy areas of Key West, people milled about at all hours. When the weather is almost always pitch-perfect it makes sense to walk around.

A skinny pale man stood two blocks away, and he was giving us more attention than a passerby should. My scan of the street continued until I found a second man that didn't fit with the scene.

"Rikki," I muttered. "We need to move."

She glanced up at me. Her eyes questioned me.

My head turned so I could check on both men. They were still standing in the same spots. With a smile at Rikki, I wanted to leave them with the impression that I hadn't seen them and everything was normal.

"Don't look, but we are being watched."

"What?" she mumbled, confused.

"Two men on either end of the street. They're out of place."

"What are they doing?" she asked, continuing to study her iPad.

"Nothing," I commented. "But it's nothing very purposefully.

"It makes sense," I pointed out. "It might confirm that this is where they found out about you."

Her eyes fumed. "Where are they?" She returned to swiping her finger on the screen of the tablet.

"One is two blocks west. The other is closer to the building."

"What do we do?"

"This will not be a repeat of yesterday," I explained. "We aren't on a deserted island. We are going to be moving amongst a lot of witnesses."

"You don't think they'll try anything?"

"Who knows?" I admitted. "They went to a lot of trouble to try and grab you yesterday, so let's assume they still want you. We just need to be ready for them."

She repeated her question, "What do we do?"

"Did you find the boy's name?" I asked.

"No, but the fisherman's last name was Altman."

Without interest, I swept my eyes over the two targets. They hadn't moved. Not professionals, I surmised.

"Are there more than two of them?" Rikki asked.

The men yesterday came in two teams. So it was logical these men would do the same.

"We weren't in the building that long," Rikki commented.

"No, they'd almost need to already be here when we arrived. Or very close."

"They work here?" she asked.

"Or they were just watching the place."

She lifted an eyebrow. "That seems like a lot of trouble," she mused.

"I'm looking forward to meeting the person putting them up to it," I admitted. "They must be sure you are onto something."

"Do we leave or what?"

I tracked both men. No change.

"Let's give it a minute. Can you find anything about a fisherman named Altman?"

She tapped her fingers across the screen and stared. Her eyes twitched left and right as she read the results.

"There is a genealogy site that shows an old picture of a Twisdale Altman standing on a small boat."

She turned the screen so I could see the picture. A weathered man in a newsboy-style cap stood in the bow of a flatboat that looked about 25 feet long. He stood over a giant grouper sprawled lifelessly on the deck of his boat.

"Does it say what year?" I asked her.

"No, but it looks like the 30s, doesn't it?"

"I can't say, but let's assume it is. Twisdale doesn't seem like a common name. So we should be able to get a hit off that."

She typed some more. Then she shook her head.

"No Twisdale."

"Obituary?" I asked. "He'd be dead by now."

"If we're judging from that picture, he died long before the internet could record it."

I shrugged. My online presence is nil; there is an email that I never check. Beyond that, there isn't enough access to steady Wi-Fi to spend a lot of time surfing the net. I'm not incapable, but if the process changes at all over a couple of years, I'm outdated.

She smiled. "Here is a Jacob Altman living in Tavernier. Along with his address and phone number."

"Are there other Altmans? That's not an unusual name."

"Yes," she admitted, "but Jacob is 94."

My lips pursed into a smile as I stated, "He might be old enough to remember something."

The two observers hadn't moved.

"Let's take this on the road," I suggested. "I want to see if they follow us."

"Where are we going to go?"

"Let's go see Jacob," I offered.

"What are we going to do about them?" Her eyes cut toward the watcher standing two blocks away.

I considered the options. Let them follow us, and one of two things will happen. They'll try to grab Rikki, or they'll try to get whatever information we know. There didn't seem to be another reason for their behavior. They wanted Rikki because she was onto something.

The question I kept asking myself, "Is it something they need or something they didn't want anyone else to learn?"

"Let's lose them," I suggested. A confrontation might go south, and they might take Rikki.

"How?"

"I haven't figured that out yet," I confessed. My hand grabbed her arm as I stood. "Let's start by heading to the car."

Rikki's bright pink Jeep was a bit of a stand-out in most places, but in Key West, a town filled with brightly-colored Jeep, scooter, and dune buggy rentals, it was just one of many. She started the engine and glanced at me.

"Duval," I told her.

She pulled off the curb, and I checked my mirrors. The two watchers converged on a truck. A Dodge. Not the stock model. It sported bigger tires and a bold Confederate flag printed on its rear window.

Rikki took the next left, heading south toward Whitehead. The truck was about six cars behind us.

"Take the next right," I said. "Try and get to the end of the street before they can follow us."

She nodded, searching ahead for the best place to turn. She took a fast turn on William Street. The engine roared as she pressed the accelerator to the floor. I lurched forward about 300 yards later when she braked to turn left. The truck was turning on William as she vanished around the corner. Again, she gunned the engine. She turned left halfway down the block on a one-way alley. Seconds later, we emerged onto Whitehead, where she turned right into the thick traffic. As we passed the Margaritaville bar, I looked back. There was no Dodge truck. I watched for several minutes before I could make it out a mile back. With the throng of pedestrians and bicycles weaving in and out of the street, it would take them forever to close the gap.

If we stayed still. We didn't. Rikki turned right on Eaton and weaved her way around the slower cars until we were pointing north.

In the rearview mirror there was no sign of the Southern boys tailing us.

8

Tavernier, Florida is an unincorporated community on Key Largo, roughly 100 miles north of Key West. It's also the longest, slowest 100 miles ever paved. Imagine following a school bus on a two-lane highway at seven in the morning. The average speed is about 41 miles per hour.

Of course, it might be one of the prettiest stretches of road. Blue water borders both sides of the highway for most of the miles. The few parts of Highway One where the ocean isn't visible are often lined with, what I would term as, Key life. Roadside shacks, colorful buildings, houses and cottages have withstood the worst that Mother Nature can fling at them.

Sure, there are some condos, chain restaurants, and a Walmart along the way. The price of paradise, I suppose. Everyone wants to visit.

After we passed through Marathon, Rikki pulled over at a small tin shack with a mural depicting a school of pompano darting among the coral. The hand-painted sign advertising the hogfish sandwich got our attention. While Rikki grabbed a picnic table, I ordered two sandwiches with two frosty glass bottles of Coca-Cola.

"Have you seen any sign of those guys?" Rikki asked as I sat down across from her.

I handed her the sweating Coke bottle and shook my head. "We lost them for now," I told her. "But, to be on the safe side, we need to keep an eye out. My gut says this is much bigger than we suspect."

"You are right," she agreed. "These guys seem too organized."

"And expendable," I pointed out. "They work for someone."

The fish shack sat on the eastern side of the highway. The ocean lapped up on the rocky shore just a few hundred feet from us; a dinghy dock extended from the coast offering cruisers and liveaboards access to fresh grilled fish. I wondered for the first time why I was tagging along with Rikki.

Rikki wasn't afraid, but she seemed to assume I was ready to jump on board this adventure. I doubted she needed me. Most people, even those who handle stressful situations well exhibit some trepidation after killing someone in self-defense. Rikki didn't seem fazed at all. The enigma of Rikki Talen intrigued me.

"A Nazi cabal?" she questioned aloud.

"White supremacist assholes don't seem to be going anywhere. The internet provides plenty of insulation and camaraderie. So it might not be that difficult to raise a small army."

"Tell me about it," she spoke with an air of sadness and defeat.

"Here's something to consider," I suggested. "You could just leave this thing alone. Get your boat back and sail someplace until it blows over."

Rikki scowled. "And let whatever asshole who's doing this get away with it. Hell no."

That response kept me tagging along. She was right: I spent over a decade fighting for freedom. My great-grandfather died in France fighting the Nazis. I didn't like that somehow they deemed it acceptable that they could reemerge. But Rikki wasn't going to back down, and I am never one to back down.

"Good," I acknowledged. "My CO used to quote, 'The only thing necessary for the triumph of evil is that good men do nothing.'"

"There are far too many people doing nothing," she admitted.

I could only agree with a nod.

An old, frail-looking man came out of the shack with two aluminum pie pans with our hogfish sandwiches. The sandwich rested on a nest of fries, sprinkled with some of the same seasonings that were on the hogfish. The first bite sent butter and juice down my chin, and I attempted to wipe it before I realized Rikki was having the same issue.

Twenty minutes later, we were back on the road. We both rode in silence, absorbed in our own thoughts. From the passenger seat, I stared out at the blue water. I wondered what Jacob Altman could tell us about a night over 80 years ago. It might prove to be a fruitless trip.

My eyes continued to check the rear-view mirror, searching for any vehicles that seemed to linger too long or showed up too often. It was a laborious task given that we were on the only road out of the Keys.

Nothing stood out, and when Rikki turned off of Highway One, I straightened, surprised that we had almost arrived.

Jacob Altman lived in the Windward Keys Assisted Living Facility. The complex operated as a nursing home and housing for seniors, complete with medical facilities and recreational areas.

A twenty-something, pony-tailed woman greeted us at the front desk. She refused to give us Altman's room number, instead she called him on the phone.

"Mr. Altman, this is Tali at the front desk. I have a couple of visitors for you."

She listened for a second before answering him. "No, sir. Their names are Chase Gordon and Rikki Talen."

He responded to her, and she looked at us, asking, "He would like you to tell me what this is about."

Rikki spoke up. "We want to talk to him about his father. We are working on some historical stories from the Keys."

It carried a ring of truth. Enough for now.

Tali hung up the phone. "He said he would meet you in the dining hall," she explained before pointing down a hallway. "It's right through those doors."

Rikki led the way as we walked into the dining hall. The room looked more like a restaurant than a nursing home dining hall. White linens covered each table, and silver flatware marked each seat. Servers walked the room greeting residents and taking orders while others brought out trays of food that looked nothing like what I would have expected.

A hostess stood at the door and greeted us. When Rikki informed her we were meeting Jacob Altman, the young woman walked us to a small round table near a picture window that stared out at the ocean. A server came by, offering us a beverage. We both opted for water while we waited.

When Altman walked in, I recognized him, or at least, his type. He walked with a firm gait compared to some other residents moving around the dining room. He was not a weak old man, and I wondered what kept the level of life in him like that.

The blond hostess escorted Altman to our table, and we both stood.

My hand extended to greet him. "Mr. Altman, my name is Chase, and this is Rikki. Thank you for taking the time to talk to us."

His grip was tight, as if he wanted to make sure I didn't underestimate him. "It's always nice to have visitors," he remarked before turning to Rikki with a sly smile. "Especially ones as pretty as you."

She returned his smile and pointed at the ring on his finger. "It looks like someone has your eye."

Altman glanced at his hand. A mixture of sadness and joy filled his eyes. "You got me," he admitted. He added, "She did, indeed. For a long time."

"How long were you married?" she asked.

"This summer would have been 75 years." His voice gave a slight crack.

The server approached. "Mr. Altman, would you like an iced tea?" he asked Altman.

"Yes, Juan," he told the man.

Altman looked us both over. "The girl said you wanted to talk to me about my father."

Rikki responded, "Yes, sir. Was your father Twisdale Altman?"

"Yes."

"And he was a fisherman?"

"As long as I can remember. The only time that man missed going out to fish was when Donna tore us up."

"Donna?" Rikki asked.

"Hurricane Donna. Back in '60, if I recall. Came ripping through here and left almost nothing on this island. Of course, we lost our house and everything, but I swear to you, Dad was more upset about *Angelica* than anything."

Rikki started to ask a question when Altman added, "His boat. *Angelica*. Damned storm demolished the entire dock. When we got back, no one ever saw hide nor hair of that girl."

"What kind of boat was she?" I asked.

"An old wooden Wheeler. With a flybridge. Might as well have been my sister the way he loved that vessel."

"Did you fish with him as a kid?" Rikki asked.

Juan returned with a glass of tea for Altman and asked if he wanted the lunch special.

"Yes, Juan," he responded. "Would you two like something to eat? Today's special is grilled pork chops with an apple demi-glaze."

"That sounds good," I told him. "But we ate a little while ago."

He nodded at me as Juan left the table.

"Yes, I spent a lot of time fishing with him–almost as soon as I could walk. He had me out hoisting lines and nets."

"Do you remember a night when he rescued a man?"

Altman's eyes brightened. "The Nazi!" he exclaimed. "Of course I remember that."

"You are sure he was a Nazi?" I questioned.

"No one was ever sure he was, but that's what everyone said. People talked about it forever. The night Twisdale Altman saved a German spy."

"Can you tell us about it?"

"Oh, sure," he started. "I was nine, and Dad and I had been out fishing since dark. We used poles and nets then. Dad was running some shrimp nets that night. When he went to pull the net in, there was a body in it. At first, he figured he caught a dolphin, but it was too light."

He took a sip of his tea and continued, "We pulled the man into the boat. I remember being scared that he was dead, but Dad got the net off him and found he was breathing. We sat him up and pulled his life preserver off him so that he would spit out the saltwater. After several minutes, he was coughing and sputtering."

"He started talking gibberish, although later I learned it was German. When Dad asked him if he was hurt, he switched to English. But his accent was terribly thick."

"What did he say?" Rikki prodded.

"He told Dad he was on a sailboat that capsized a few days earlier. I assumed Dad trusted him about that. I was young and figured he was an adult, and adults never lie."

"Boy, was I wrong, right?" He chuckled to himself. "After all these years, I can understand. He wouldn't be floating around like that for days."

"Your dad didn't believe him, though?"

"He was wearing a uniform, like a jumpsuit. I remembered there was a name on it. Vogel. I had no idea what it meant. Dad figured it was his name, even though he told us his name was Richman. Henry Richman. And he was clutching a box that weighed 50 to 60 pounds. Dad said later that he was in a life raft or something that capsized. Figured he was off some German U-boat trying to bomb the base."

"What happened to him?" I asked.

"Back then we didn't have radios on the boat. We had to get back to shore before we could call the authorities. Dad used to tell the story that he had his hand on his old .38 the entire trip home. I had no clue. He told me to clean the fish. I realize now that he wanted me doing something out of reach of the man. It worried him that Richman or Vogel would get his strength back. That he might have a gun in that box and would kill us both in order to take the boat."

"Why didn't he just restrain him?" Rikki asked.

"Dad was never very forceful. He didn't like confrontation. Partly why he spent so much time alone fishing, no one to deal with."

We both listened to every word and intonation. Altman's genial tone made him a natural raconteur.

"Don't get me wrong," Altman clarified. "I know he would have killed the man if he presented any danger to me."

Rikki leaned forward. "What happened when you got to shore?"

"We tied up, and Dad told me to run to the store. We had a little bait shop and general store. Mr. Abernathy ran it, and he was opening up when I showed up. This had to be around four or five. I told him that Dad wanted him to call the sheriff because we rescued a man."

"Mr. Abernathy and a couple of men that were in the store walked me back to the docks. Dad said the man just walked away. He didn't hurt him, and Dad didn't stop him. He just disappeared."

"When the sheriff arrived, it was almost morning. They searched for him, but there was no sign of him. He might have gotten to the road and caught a ride, but no one ever heard."

"That's incredible," I told him. "Did anyone ever find out what was in the box?"

Altman's smile was shrewd. "No, but Dad always suspected. The next night when he went out fishing, he found a gold coin in one of his tackle boxes. The coin was engraved with an eagle and Swastika."

Rikki cut her eyes to me. We both sat, transfixed in the moment. Then, after several seconds, Rikki asked, "What did your father do with it?"

Altman laughed. "The old man couldn't spend it. Dad was already becoming the subject of gossip for rescuing a Nazi. The last thing he wanted was anyone to suspect he got paid to do it. He never got too wrapped up in the patriotism that swept the nation during those days. Not that he didn't love his country, but he often said that people who talk the loudest about things are just pretending.

"But it was pure gold. So he ended up melting it down into nuggets and carrying it up to Miami. He told me later that he got about $50 for it, which was quite a lot back in those days."

"That's the only one you saw?" Rikki asked with fervent attention.

Altman, still smiling, gave her a close examination. "There's more out there?" he asked. "I suppose you are going to find it?"

Rikki glanced at me for a second. I responded, "Yes, Mr. Altman."

His head tossed back in laughter. It was hard to tell if it was humor he found in us or the whole situation. After catching his breath, saying, "I knew it. I used to search the woods after that, hoping that Vogel hid the treasure somewhere."

"Every kid's dream, isn't it?" I commented.

"Hell, yes!" Altman blurted. "Did he hide it somewhere?"

"We aren't sure," Rikki asserted. "Do you remember where you rescued Vogel?"

"Sweetie, I was a kid. I don't have any idea."

"Do you remember what size engine *Angelica* had back then?" I asked.

"That was an old steam engine," Altman mused. "It would top out at about 20 knots."

"How fast did your father run it that night?"

"Oh, that's one of the few nights I recall him running it full on. He was in a hurry to get to shore."

Rikki studied me before she asked the next question. "How long do you remember it taking to get back to shore?"

"Oh, I was just a kid," Altman pointed out. "Time is so relative to a child. It felt like forever, but I bet it was only a couple of hours."

The old man looked back and forth at us. Finally, his words came out with his realization. "You suppose that there's more treasure where we picked him up?"

"It's a long shot," Rikki admitted.

Altman grinned. "Sounds like an awesome shot, though."

The senior was hard not to like. He had 94 years of stories, and he was missing those adventures now.

"Come to think of it," he added, "You aren't the only ones looking for it."

Rikki cocked her head. "What do you mean?"

"Last year, this man came to see me." He glanced at Rikki before stating, "A real asshole. Pardon my French, dear."

She waved off his apology and asked, "What did he want?"

"Oh, he asked about the man we rescued. He asked the same question: where did we rescue him?"

I lifted an eyebrow and leaned forward. "Do you remember his name?"

"Oh, yes. I didn't like him. Something about him made my skin crawl," he explained. "I pulled the old dementia bit. Pretended to forget where I was. Acted like he was my brother."

His attention turned toward Rikki with a proud smile. "It's quite a shtick," he joked. "This man was getting frustrated, trying to explain who he was. After I frustrated him for long enough he admitted his name was Paul Richman, and that Henry Richman was his grandfather."

"What did you tell him?" Rikki asked.

"Nothing," Altman informed her. "I told you, I didn't trust him. So I played out my act until he left."

Rikki stared into his eyes for a second. "Do you trust us?"

Altman shrugged. "I didn't get that prickly feeling about you two," he told her. "And there was something about the way you reminded me of Brenda. You didn't try to beguile me."

Rikki flashed a white smile, stating, "No, but I can spot someone who can't be beguiled."

"Every smart woman can," he replied.

The server appeared with Altman's plate of pork chops as I stared out the window at the sea.

"I say, though," he remarked, "I hope you two will come back and let me know how this ends. Nothing beats a good treasure hunt tale."

"Except," he amended, "a damned good bottle of single barrel."

9

By the time we left the Windward Keys Assisted Living Facility, the sun was on a steady descent. Jacob Altman regaled us with stories from his life. How he met Brenda, two tours in Korea, and several marvelous stories of working on a mail boat that ran from the Keys to the Exumas. He shared anecdotes about how the Keys sprouted through their development and tourism.

By two, he thanked us for our time, wished us luck in our adventure, and excused himself for what he referred to as a pre-dinner nap.

"Paul Richman?" Rikki asked aloud as we stepped back into the tropical sun.

"Seems interesting," I responded. "What can you find out about him?"

She slid behind the wheel of her Jeep and before she fastened her seat belt, she pulled out her iPad. "I'm already ahead of you," she commented.

Inside of three minutes, she began reading the data she found. The girl seemed to dig through the internet like she knew right where that tidbit of information was hiding.

"There's a Paul Richman living on Sugarloaf Key. Looks like he's a lawyer."

My brow furrowed. "Can you determine if he's related to our Henry Richman?"

She suggested, "If he is the grandson of the Henry Richman that the Altmans saved, I can try to work backwards. Unfortunately, there wasn't enough information from the '40s to determine who Henry Richman was."

"We're looking at three hours back to Key West," I pointed out. "If I remember, Sugarloaf Key is somewhere north of there."

Rikki cut her eyes at me. "Isn't everything somewhere north of Key West," she quipped.

With a smirk, I replied, "Yeah, yeah. I mean I think it's closer to Key West than it is to here."

"What are you thinking?"

My index finger touched the rear-view mirror as I studied the clouds floating across the sky behind me. "Those good old boys we ran across this morning are going to be looking for us," I explained, "or you, to be more precise."

She turned her head toward me as I spoke.

"They won't have a lot of trouble finding out what hotel we are staying at," I continued. "Given that they know your name and, no doubt, mine by now."

"We shouldn't go back," she stated.

"Not yet, at least," I agreed. "When we are ready to be found, we can go back."

"We can find a motel along the way," she suggested. "Do you have any cash?"

"You're kidding, right?" I stared at her. "I didn't even have clothes until you bought them for me."

A sly grin appeared on her lips. "I guess you are at my beck and call."

I ignored her jest. "Let's assume that whoever is behind this can track us."

She nodded.

"The safest course is to lead them away from where we plan to go."

Rikki looked out at the road and said, "North?"

"It'll take about an hour to get to Homestead." I detailed my idea. "We use your credit card to book a room and get some cash. After that, we head south and stay off the radar."

"That's a lot of trouble," she replied.

"And it might not help at all."

"They could be tracking my phone," she thought aloud. "In which case, it won't matter."

After a quick glance around the parking lot, I shook my head. "I don't think so. We've been here for several hours talking to Jacob. If they were tracking us with any sort of GPS tracker, even a phone, we'd have company by now."

"But there's no guarantee they are tracking my card, either."

"If it would make you feel better, we could toss your phone on the next bus to Orlando."

She curled her lip at me as her phone buzzed in her pocket.

"It's the hospital," she announced as she answered the phone.

While she spoke to whoever was calling, I stared off at the ocean, trying not to listen.

I heard her say, "Thank you," before she hung up.

"Sam's out of surgery," she confirmed. "He's stable but still critical."

"What's next for him?"

"He has a niece who's on her way down to be with him. They have to re-evaluate his condition. They had to relieve the swelling on his brain, and now it's a 'wait and see' time. If he doesn't go downhill, there will be more surgeries."

"I'm sorry."

"I'm going to make these people pay for this," she vowed.

"We gotta find them first," I pointed out. I brightened, saying, "I imagine, when it's all said and done, they are going to regret crossing you."

"Damned straight," she whistled as she started the engine. "Homestead, huh?"

"It might make them look for us on the mainland."

She paused. "You don't think that they'll make another run at Sam to get to me."

I shook my head. "I doubt it. There's not much they can do to him at this point. As long as he's in the hospital, he should be safe."

We spent the next few hours making the trek north, checking into a hotel and, with only a stop for gas, turning around to head south.

As we crossed the Everglades, Rikki mused aloud, "Vogel escapes whatever the fate that befell the rest of his comrades, right?"

"Sure," I agreed. "The ship is going down, and he does what most people do. Save their own ass."

"But," she added, "he knows that there is a shit ton of gold. Why only save yourself, when you can also get rich doing it?"

"It says a lot about the man. He's thinking ahead."

"We're supposing a lot of things though."

"Without knowing the fate of the mission, we are. He might have had plenty of time to plan it. Vogel might have waited for the right moment to grab some gold and jump ship."

"But how much could he carry?" Rikki pondered. "A box of gold isn't light. Even an extra 20 pounds is going to drag him under. Jacob said the box he held was about 50 pounds. It'd be tough to tread water with that much weight."

"He was wearing a life jacket," I pointed out.

"Still, that would have been exhausting."

"How much would 50 pounds of gold be worth?" I asked.

"Jacob said his father got about $50 for one coin."

"Let's say one coin weighed an ounce, and let's round down to $30 per coin. That would be about 800 coins. So a rough estimate would be $24,000."

Rikki did some math in her head before saying, "That's equivalent to $200,000 today."

"Are you kidding?" I questioned her. "That's a lot."

"Give or take," she amended.

"That's a lot of incentive," I considered.

"Enough to stay afloat, I guess."

"He'd have a healthy new start," I commented. "Fast forward to now, and his grandson wants to find the remaining treasure that his grandfather left behind."

"Is he the one sending the racist assholes after us?" she questioned.

"Let's go have a talk with him tomorrow."

10

Sugarloaf Key lies about halfway between Marathon and Key West. If one were looking on an atlas, there would be an Upper Sugarloaf Key and Lower Sugarloaf Key, but that seemed to only matter to people that lived on the respective islands.

Paul Richman lived on the eastern edge of Lower Sugarloaf Key. The house was built on the edge of a cliff overlooking the ocean below. A wrought-iron fence stretched a quarter-mile down the road. The property appeared to be about ten acres of prime oceanfront land. Someone carved an inlet out of the cliff to create a protected dock.

The drive to the fortress curved along the edge of the island. Richman was a man of some means. Experience had taught me that men like that had very little qualms about squashing whatever gets in their way. We were about to announce our presence to him.

I considered cautioning Rikki about my concerns. Her face tightened, and her teeth were grinding. She was already on the same page as me.

The door opened, and a fake-tanned man in a polo shirt and khaki pants opened the door. Something about a man that sits around in khakis at his house gives me pause. He was mid-50s, and he was fighting, with some success, to stave off the effects of aging. The man colored his hair to hide the graying, but the effect was subtle, making it almost unnoticeable. It was the beard color that was just a shade off that clued me. A seamless tan, something on the spectrum of well-oiled teak, covered his skin, which he also kept well-oiled.

"Can I help you?" he asked as he studied both of us. His eyes crawled past us to take in the pink Jeep parked in his circular drive.

"Yes, sir," Rikki responded, offering a congenial smile that few could resist. Her hand extended, and Richman grasped it out of habit. Genteel people respond to proper greetings. Society ingrained it in him. I almost smiled at how fast Rikki reeled him.

"My name is Rikki. I'm doing some historical research, and I'm wondering if we could talk to you for a minute."

His pupils widened a bit. "About what?"

"Can we have a few minutes to explain it?"

Richman gave her a scan with his eyes. He realized she pulled him into her comfort zone, and now he wanted to retreat. Curiosity, though, crossed his face.

"I only have a few minutes," he conceded.

Before he could change, or even set, the terms, Rikki took a subtle step forward. Again, Richman responded out of habit. He stepped back as she moved forward, allowing her entry.

"What kind of history are you researching?" he asked again.

"Some local legends and such."

"I'm not sure how I can help you," he offered as a feigned apologetic statement.

"You have a great place," I told him as we entered the foyer. The floor was a marble slab. Crisp black and white photographs of the ocean adorned the walls. A floral aroma wafting from the various arrangements in the room hung in the air.

"Thank you." Richman ushered us into a living room with a picture window that overlooked the ocean. His discomfort was apparent. He didn't mean to let us intrude, and somehow, still, he didn't want to turn us away.

"Is that a de Havilland?" I asked, pointing down toward the protected dock.

A blue and yellow seaplane was berthed next to a 40-foot yacht.

"Yes," he boasted, "1952. She is a complete refit."

"She's beautiful," I praised. "How often do you take her out?"

He moved over next to me by the window. His chest heaved out as I admired the plane.

"Few times a week. I fly her back and forth to the islands. When I have to head back to New York, I have a Swearingen over at Summerland Airport."

"Very nice," I admitted, my head bobbing with approval.

"You fly?" he asked.

"Not in far too many years," I confessed. "My uncle taught me when I was 12. He had an old Piper that he restored. I never got a license, but that didn't stop me from logging as many hours as possible. My family figured I'd end up in the Air Force when I turned 18."

His gaze drifted over to my shoulder. "Looks like you took a different direction."

I shrugged. "Fate, I suppose."

He shook off the camaraderie we shared for a brief second. "What is it I can help you with?" He turned his attention back to Rikki.

"We are interested in your grandfather, Henry Richman."

His eyebrow twitched up. "My grandfather? He was from New York."

"Is that so?" Rikki sat in a high-back chair. She crossed her legs with intent and grace, rested her hands on her knees, and leaned forward at a slight angle. "What kind of business did he do?"

"He was in finance," he explained. "He started his own company after the war. Offered loans and mortgages to returning soldiers."

"Where was he born?" Rikki prodded.

"Canada," Richman replied. "A little town just north of Niagara. I forget the name. He moved to New York long before I was around."

"And your grandmother?" Rikki asked. "Where did they meet?"

I moved away from the window and walked along behind the two as they talked.

Richman answered, "She was the daughter of a customer. She came in to pay a loan for her father, and my grandfather invited her to dinner. They got married a few months later."

"Did he forgive the loan?" I joked.

"I wouldn't be privy to that." Richman glared at me, and I guessed I was pushing a boundary. Best to let Rikki do the talking, I decided.

"How long were they married?" Rikki interjected, saving the line of questioning.

"He died in '92. She just passed two years ago."

As Rikki interrogated him, I studied his bookshelf. His collection included a spattering of leather-bound classics, a few political commentaries leaning toward the conservative right, and a couple of travel books.

My eyes fell on two books. *The 88 Principle* and *Reclaiming Our Path*. All the titles were bold, block letters that stretched around the spines. "Wexler" was printed on the bottom of each spine. The author, I assumed.

There was an urge to pull either of them from the shelf. I resisted. Richman was already glancing over his shoulder at me with some annoyance.

"What do you want with my grandfather?" Richman blurted out.

Rikki's mouth turned up in a small smile, offering a gentle, passive demeanor as she steadied her aim. "We've been doing some research, tracking a German naval officer named Vogel that might have come into the States back in 1940."

"What does that have to do with my grandfather?"

"I suspect Vogel changed his name to Henry Richman."

"That's bullshit!" Richman jumped to his feet. "How dare you accuse my family of being Nazis?"

"Mr. Richman," I commented in a hushed tone, "no one is saying that. If anything, it would seem that Vogel defected from the Reich."

His chest heaved in and out as he fumed. "You come into my house... My house!" he exploded. "To call my grandfather a Nazi."

"Mr. Richman," Rikki started.

He put his hand up, stopping the next word. "Don't!"

Her lips pursed. She didn't continue.

Richman pointed at the door. "I want you both out of here. I don't like the direction you're going with this 'research.'" His fingers signaled air quotes. "If you try to make any such egregious claims, I'll sue the shit out of you. Libel, slander, whatever it takes. I'll drag you through court and make damned sure that you come out of it broken and battered."

Rikki rose to her feet. "I'm sorry, Mr. Richman," she offered.

His cheeks were growing redder.

"Come on." I urged Rikki toward the door.

The man wasn't going to give us anything else. The door echoed as he slammed it behind us.

"That was fruitless," she mumbled when we got back into the Jeep.

"Not really," I disagreed.

She glanced over at me.

"That was over the top, don't you think?"

She nodded.

"I mean," I started, "he could have denied it, or even played it off as surprise. 'The family didn't talk that much about my grandfather's birthplace.' Or even show a bit of disbelief."

"Instead, it was all grandiose. Threats of lawsuits, which doesn't mean much from a lawyer. It's a little like being surprised that a dog licks his balls. It's what they do."

"So, Vogel is his grandfather?" she questioned as she started the Jeep.

"Oh, yeah, and he knows it," I confirmed. "Let me see your phone."

She handed it to me, and I opened the search app and typed "Wexler. *88 Principle*."

"Aha," I surmised when the results came up.

"What?"

"Richman had a couple of books on his shelf. The *88 Principle* and one called *Reclaiming Our Path*. Both of those books were written and published by Daniel Wexler, a self-claimed Nazi. According to his website here, he states he adheres to the original principles of the Nazis."

"Hmm, that's crazy," I added. "He runs Nazi tours out of Tampa. You can book tours to Germany, France, any place with A significant history to the Third Reich."

"Damn," Rikki whistled.

"It was the 88 in the title," I explained.

"Of course," she interrupted. "H is the eighth letter in the alphabet. The 88 stands for '*Heil Hitler*.'"

I nodded. "He started getting antsy when I was near that part of the bookshelf.

"Did he send those guys after me?" she wondered.

"He seems like the best candidate," I admitted. "We surprised him. Like we were out of place, meaning he might have known who we were when we showed up, though. Just a hunch."

"Why would he let us in?"

"We caught him off-guard. He wondered how we got there," I explained. "Why we showed up at his door."

"He has known about the gold his entire life," she mused. "Bedtime stories from Grandpa about a submarine full of gold somewhere between Florida and Cuba."

"When you poked around the records and found the police report, he wanted to find out what you had discovered. Especially since Jacob didn't give him anything worthwhile."

Rikki shook her head in disbelief.

After a second, she turned to look at me. "I need a drink," she announced.

"Sounds good to me. Just make sure I can grab a burger there."

11

Rikki picked the place for lunch. Her tastes seemed to run the gamut. For a girl born with a silver spoon in her mouth, she didn't seem to fit in that world. Not firmly, at least.

She could dress the part, know the correct words to use, as well as the appropriate fork, and flutter her eyelashes like a debutante. But that wasn't her, and I liked the spitfire attitude that was lurking under the surface.

When she pulled off the highway, my eyes were watching a cloud roll around the sky. Meanwhile, my mind was twirling around random thoughts, trying to make sense of the people who were after Rikki.

I've witnessed some horrible things during my time in the Corps and in the years since I got out that gave me pause to think. People willing to do anything because of a belief.

Women and children were willing to strap an explosive to themselves in the name of their ideology. I've never understood it. Ideology, religion, or whatever beliefs that make up a person's background are important. But for those beliefs to culminate in death and mayhem seems to me to be a disconnect.

No time in history has force ever legitimized any ideology. It seems to be counterintuitive. Yet, whether the perpetrator is blowing up an abortion clinic in the name of Jesus or driving a van filled with C-4 into a mall in the name of Allah, the result is increased opposition. There is no conversion, simply elimination.

What's the end result: Hitler couldn't kill all the Jews; instead, he brought about his own downfall by rallying the world against him. Likewise, Al-Qaeda didn't eliminate the heathen Western world on 9/11; it only woke up America to its existence.

People like Richman or the Wexler-guy live in a world filled with hate, and I didn't understand it. I can't say I've never hated an individual, but never a group. I've had to kill, but never out of hate.

Why is it we've evolved so far in so many areas, but still this idiotic mindset still exists that somehow one group of people is better than another? Was it possible that my own beliefs drove me to do things that were as misguided? Had the wave of patriotism that spawned after 9/11 given way to the religion of America? Were the battles and wars that ensued nothing more than a religious war?

That's where my mind wandered until the crunch of gravel under the tires pulled me from that unending mire. Rikki pulled the Jeep up to a cinder-block building with a neon sign saying, "Burger Yard."

"You said you wanted a burger," she told me as she cut the engine.

"I was getting peckish," I confirmed.

"After dealing with that asshole, I just want a shot of whiskey."

The Burger Yard was a bar with six small round tables scattered around the small room, a ten-foot bar stretching along the back wall. This was a local joint, not some tourist spot filled with pictures of Jimmy Buffett or Mick Jagger, when they stopped off. There were no windows to show off the vistas or even let a ray of natural light into the room. A handful of half-lit florescent-tubed fixtures, a flat screen and one big projection television that was at least 20 years old illuminated the room. Both televisions were playing SportsCenter. Jethro Tull filled the dark bar with *Aqualung*, one of the strangest songs I could think of right at that moment.

"Bar or table?" she asked.

"Always the bar," I told her. "No point in making the bartender walk around for us."

She shrugged and pulled out a stool.

Various liquors filled the shelves behind the bar. Not the high-end varietals. No Ciroc or Aviation, just Stoli and Tanqueray. The bartender looked like he was the owner. He was pushing 50, and he looked like he was born and raised in the Conch Republic. Those locals are easy to spot after a while, they have an assured sense of place here. Like Jacob, born and raised in the Keys.

"What can I get you?" He ambled up to us.

"Two shots of that Old Charter," Rikki told him.

"And a burger."

He gave a curt nod. "Burgers come with cheese, onions, pickles, and mustard. You want chips?"

"Sounds divine," I told him.

"How about you?" he asked Rikki.

"I'm drinking my lunch."

He filled two shot glasses with the bourbon before moving to the flat griddle and tossing a beef patty on to the hot surface. The sizzle was audible over both SportsCenter and the music.

"Cheers," I toasted, clinking our shot glasses before tossing them back.

The gloomy bar brightened for a second as the metal door opened. A shaft of light cut across the room, reflected into a mirrored Coors Light sign, and bounced across the room at an angle. The door slammed shut, vanquishing the rays that made it through for a second.

In the Coors Light mirror, I noted three burly bikers standing by the door. They didn't speak to each other, but one pointed at a table in the corner.

Before the hairs on the back of my neck stood all the way up, Rikki whispered, "Shit."

She was right. My instinct muttered the same thing as soon as I saw them. I twisted on my stool toward Rikki so that I could get a better look at them.

"Recognize them?" I questioned under my breath.

"No, just the way they looked at me."

"Maybe it's nothing," I tried to assure her.

It wasn't. They all were watching her. Not overtly. They were talking amongst themselves. Their words were inaudible. My years working behind a bar gave me some insight. Guys like this didn't talk at respectable levels. When they walk into a bar, they want to be noticed. The decibels of their voices ramp up, and if no one pays them attention, then they just get rowdier.

Not these guys. They hadn't yelled at the bartender for a beer yet. No boasting about their ride in. Just a quiet, intimate conversation between them.

I used a quick turn of my head to appraise the three. They were rough, and judging from the scars I saw on all three of their faces, they didn't mind fighting.

The big giveaway was how strained they were in avoiding staring at Rikki. In a tight area like this, it would be hard not to notice someone like Rikki. Instead, all three of them kept their eyes on each other.

"What do we do?" Ricki asked.

I didn't answer. Instead, I was sorting out the hierarchy. Who was the dominant one? Finally, I decided it was the shortest of the three. He sported a bushy beard and crooked nose. He faced me and looked like he was doing most of the talking.

The bartender walked over to them. I heard them order three bottles of Miller Lite. Simple tastes.

When the bartender returned behind the bar, he pulled my burger off the grill and slid it onto a bun.

"Enjoy," he told me as he put the burger in front of me.

I sighed, trying to decide if I take the time to eat or not.

Rikki glanced from me to the burger. She seemed to know what I was thinking.

"I think you have time," she told me.

My eyes cut toward the bikers, who were getting their beers at that moment. With the burger requiring two hands, I took a big bite out of it. The cheese and grease oozed out of the other side, dropping to the plate in a congealed mess.

Rikki started talking, "If they are going to be a problem, then we need to split them up."

I swallowed and stared at her for a second. "What?"

She bounced off the chair, patted my cheek with her hand, and stated, "I'm going to the ladies' room."

As she crossed behind me, her fingertips dragged across my shoulders, sending an electric charge through me. My head turned, of its own accord, to watch her walk away. She passed the end of the bar and disappeared down a narrow corridor with a sign reading "Head" on the wall.

I took another bite of my burger and twisted on my stool. The three bikers were conspiring. At least one of their eyes cut my way every few seconds. I focused my attention on the tube TV playing sports highlights.

One biker stood up with every effort to appear casual. He started moving toward the hallway that Rikki had just vanished down.

With his arms crossed, the bartender was leaning against the back bar and watching the television. At least mostly. His eyes moved around as he absorbed everything.

"Can I get a Coors Light?" I asked.

Without moving more than his left arm, he opened the cooler and retrieved a bottle of beer.

"Don't open it yet," I told him.

He took a second to shrug before setting the beer in front of me.

I straightened on the stool as one of the other bikers rose and approached the bar. He was the one I pegged as being "in charge." He ambled over.

"Hey," he blurted out to the bartender. "Three more beers."

The bartender turned to grab the bottles.

"Where ya from?" he questioned me.

"Nowhere particular," I responded. My fingers were dancing around the neck of the unopened beer bottle.

"Pretty girl you got there," he sneered.

I sighed a heavy breath.

The biker's beady eyes narrowed at me. "You got a problem?" he hissed.

"Are we doing this now?" I pondered.

"Doing what?"

"You making crude sexist comments to get a rise out of me."

"What the hell are you talking about?"

"Where'd your buddy go?" I asked.

He let the corners of his lips lift in a sadistic grin. My eyes cut to the bartender who had enough experience in a roadhouse to sense danger. I wondered what his move was going to be. My gut said he would step out of the way for the moment. He'd wait until it became his fight before he stepped in.

"I figured as much," I commented to Bushy Beard.

His face came close to mine. "Don't worry," he promised, "he won't do any permanent damage."

I returned his smile. "I can't promise that she won't."

His eyes flashed with confusion, and he made a mistake. He glanced at his buddy still seated 15 feet away. My right hand shot up. My fingers entwined into his beard, and I jerked the biker's face into the bar. A resounding crunch emitted from his face, and as his head bounced off the wooden surface, my left hand swung the unopened Coors Light bottle against his temple.

Beer bottles break much easier when they are full and capped. I don't know the actual physics behind it, but I've dropped enough empty and unopened ones behind the bar to know it works. While not based on any objective scientific evidence, I have found that the empties bounce 99 times out of 100. The unopened ones shatter almost every time.

This one shattered, sending beer and glass shards all over his face. My arm pulled him down again, slamming his face into the bar a second time. He went limp and dribbled to the floor like a puddle of water.

His friend bounded to his feet as soon as Bushy Beard's face hit the bar for the first time. He hadn't made it around the table by the time Bushy Beard was in a pool of wasted machismo on the floor.

"You son of a bitch," he howled as he lunged across the room at me.

His right arm pulled a four-inch hunting knife from a sheath on his back belt loop. He would not be as unprepared as his friend. With my barstool outstretched like a javelin, I charged him. The blade swiped toward me, but the stool drove into his chest. A gasp of wind rushed out of his lungs. He stumbled back when I shoved the seat forward like a battering ram, forcing him across the barroom. The stool fell to the ground as I grabbed one of the empty bottles of beers he had left at his table.

The bottle stunned him when it hit his temple.

It didn't break, though. It was empty.

My hand caught the wrist of the hand still wielding the hunting knife. My thumb dug into the point where the radius and ulna bones connect. His hand flexed as I found the pressure point. Brushing the blade out of his hand, I let it hit the floor before I kicked it away from him.

He was recovering his breath, and I didn't want him to find a second wind. I dropped his wrist and drove my right fist into his throat. My left followed with a blow to his chest, stunning him further.

Time to end it. My right foot drove down onto his knee. The force buckled his leg the wrong way. He bellowed in pain as he fell into a fetal position, trying to grasp his shattered knee.

He would have a limp for the rest of his life. I turned to see the bartender standing back. He gave me a quick nod, and I ran down the hall toward the ladies' room.

The door slammed against the wall as I threw my shoulder into it.

Rikki stood next to a broken sink. The corner of the wall-mounted sink was lying on the floor next to the bloodied head of the biker. After a quick double-take, I could see the blood bubbling out of his nose. He was breathing.

Rikki glanced at the mirror, nonchalantly wiped a droplet of blood off her cheek, and walked out of the bathroom.

12

The bartender weighed the options of whether to call the police, but when Rikki offered him a thousand bucks to cover the expense of repairs, he opted to let the bikers find their own way out.

"I guess that clinches it," I pointed out as she drove south toward Key West. "We know Richman is involved."

She nodded. "Seems too convenient, doesn't it?

"Maybe the fluorescent pink Jeep was a giveaway, too?" I questioned her. "A new ride might help us stay below the radar."

"Screw that," she howled. "I love my Jeep, and I found that a little fun."

Her phone buzzed on the console before I had a chance to disagree with her.

She answered, and I returned my gaze to the passing scenery.

"You mind if we make a stop?" she asked.

I shrugged. "I'm on your dime."

"Sam's awake and out of surgery."

"Was that him?"

She shook her head. "His niece. She said he was asking about me."

"You two are close, huh?" I noted.

"Yes," she admitted. "He's been around since I was a kid. He was always working for my dad in some aspect. Always taking care of me."

"Your very own Alfred."

She cut her eyes at me. "Cute," she snapped at a joke she had heard a hundred times.

"He's more like my only friend," she confessed. "Stupid, I guess. I never take the time to get to know anyone. Sam's just always been around. He's easy."

"Is he going to be okay?" I asked.

"I'm not sure." Her tone shook. Nervous. She had been running hard to avoid worrying about him, and now she was slowing down.

It was one of the first real cracks in her veneer. She'd lured that biker into the bathroom with no hesitation. She shot and killed the Nazi on Little Pine Key without a thought. Now she was fighting back the tears in worry. There were layers of guilt added on there. The attack on Sam was an attempt to get to her, and she felt responsible. There was no dissuading that notion, either. It wasn't her fault, but it was an anchor she was going to tote around for a bit.

After seeing the biker in the bathroom, I didn't envy the man responsible for Sam Cornell's condition. Rikki had a vendetta.

The Florida Keys Memorial Hospital was on the north side of the island. Rikki and I found our way up to the ICU, where Becca, Sam's niece, was waiting for us. Becca Cornell had fiery red hair that twisted like corkscrews just past her shoulder. She was a few years older than me. Her skin was smooth and pale, but she looked like there was a tough center to her.

"How is he?" Rikki asked her as soon as their hug ended.

"Sam's got a long road, but the doctor thinks he should recover. His lung collapsed, and he had so many broken bones. They have him in traction, so he won't be moving much for a few days."

"Have the police been by?" I asked.

Becca glanced at me with some trepidation. Who was I?

She nodded after a second. "Yes, but the detective said that he would be back when Uncle Sam was feeling a little better."

"Can I see him?" Rikki asked. She was walking along a razor's edge, weighing her own feelings and relationship with Sam to that of his actual family. She was envious of Becca. Not even aware of it. Rikki wanted validation of her feelings.

"Yes," Becca said, tossing another sideways glance at me. "You guys can go in. I'll go grab a coffee."

"Come on," Rikki urged, taking my hand.

She led me through the swinging doors, where she spoke to the nurse guarding the entrance. A nurse directed us to a corner room where we found Sam Cornell sleeping. The television hanging on the opposite wall was playing a cartoon. Something innocuous for him to sleep to, I guessed.

Rikki touched his arm with her fingertips. "Sam," she whispered.

The man opened his eyes and blinked a few times. "Rikki, love," he croaked.

"Hey there." She smiled at him.

His words slurred together, no doubt a symptom of the pain-killers the staff were filling him with. "You're safe," he mumbled. "I didn't mean to..."

"You didn't," she reassured him.

His glassy eyes examined me. He tried to mouth a question, but Rikki stopped him.

"Sam, this is Chase," she introduced me. "He helped me with those bastards that did this to you."

The man blinked. There was a look in those eyes. A desire to grill me the way a father might before a suitor took his little girl off to the movies. The drugs and injuries exhausted him too much, though.

"He's okay," she assured him. "I promise."

"He better be." His voice strained.

His fingers extended, and Rikki grasped them.

"Myloader," he mumbled. "Go see him."

"What?" she questioned.

"Milo. Oder." He spoke slower.

"Who is he?"

"A friend," Sam stuttered. "In Miami."

The IV hissed and whirred as it pumped another round of meds into his bloodstream. His eyes lolled around as he tried to focus them on Rikki. To no avail.

He muttered, "Goadasee'em" before drifting back into a Dilaudid fueled slumber.

"Who's Milo Oder?" I asked Rikki.

She pursed her lips and shook her head.

"I'm going to step out," I offered. "You sit with him for a bit."

She gave me an appreciative smile, and I left her to her bedside vigil.

Becca sat in the waiting room. She had one of those tiny Styrofoam coffee cups that seem to be more frustrating than satisfying. The television featured some make-believe judge ruling on a ludicrous dispute between two people with the collective brain cells of an amoeba. The quality of this kind of entertainment reminded me why I prefer an isolated cove with a novel by John MacDonald.

"You might need a refill," I suggested to Becca.

She glanced inside her cup and sighed. "Yeah, I am desperate for some." There were remnants of a faint accent. Something that she had spent a lot of time hiding.

"Rikki's going to be back there a bit," I told her. "Why don't I buy you a cup of coffee at the cafeteria?"

She smiled. "Sure. I hate this powdered cream, anyway."

Becca led me to the elevator that took us down to the cafeteria.

"How do you know Rikki?" she asked after we found a table.

"We just met," I answered.

She lifted an eyebrow–some curiosity mixed with caution.

I explained, "The day of the attack. I happened to be in the wrong place. Or the right one, depending on your point of view."

"What happened?" she queried.

"It seems Rikki was being targeted. I intervened."

"'Intervened,'" she questioned. "What does that mean?"

"I stopped their attack by means of physical confrontation."

"Physical confrontation?"

"It's the preferable term," I told her. "'Kicked their asses' is a more accurate description."

"Do you tend to 'intervene?'" she asked.

"The United States government spent a lot of money training me to intervene," I commented.

Becca nodded at my tattoo. "I noticed the brand."

"It's a hard habit to break."

"I did a stint in the Navy," she stated. "Two tours in the Gulf."

"It does stay with you. So what do you do now?"

She responded, "I'm in advertising," she responded "Most of the time I design graphics for billboards and signs."

I sipped my coffee and bobbed my head.

"Is 'intervening' your full-time job?" she asked me.

"No, I try to avoid work. But when I do need money, I work as a bartender for a hotel up in West Palm Beach."

"You spend a lot of time in the sun," she noted, looking at my browned arms.

"I live on a sailboat."

"Wow." Her eyes widened. "How do you do that?"

"The same way anyone lives anywhere." I continued, "The boat is like a house or an apartment. While I was in the Corps, I didn't have to pay for my living arrangements. When I got out, I had this nice little nest egg. When I'm up in West Palm, I keep *Carina*, that's my boat, berthed at the marina where I work. Otherwise, I'm anchored out somewhere for free. Not a lot of expenses that way."

"That sounds amazing," she admitted. "I don't think I could do that."

I've heard the same thing from many people. People love the idea of a dream like sailing the islands for the rest of their lives, and as long as they think it's unattainable, then it can stay "the dream." Often, they never take the plunge out of fear. That's true for most dreams. Fear of failing. Fear of hating it. Fear of other people's opinions.

"Do you have any family?" she asked.

"Yeah," I responded. "My mother and my sister live up in North Arkansas. We don't talk much. My mother was a rolled-in-red, die-hard Conservative. She thought joining the Marines was the height of my failures. They expected me to go to college, work for some big company, and move back to the farm to take care of her."

"You grew up on a farm?"

"No," I laughed, "I just mean, she wanted me close to her so that someone could take care of her."

"What about your sister?"

"She can't take care of herself," I said. "My mother raised her to do one thing: marry someone who would take care of her. Which is strange, given that my mom couldn't do that herself."

Becca nodded.

I felt my face flush. "Sorry," I muttered, "I got on a roll."

She laughed, "No, that's fine. I'm pretty close to my mom. My dad died when I was a baby, so it was just my mom."

"What about Sam?"

Becca's face twisted into an awkward smile. "Sam was great, but he just wasn't there much. He was always away. With Rikki or her father."

"She seems very fond of him."

"Yeah," she answered.

She didn't try to hide the envy, even though it didn't seem to consume her. The irony of it was that both women envied the other. I could have pointed it out to Becca, but I doubt it would make a difference. They were like sisters, always wondering which one was the favorite.

"I guess we need to head back," Becca commented.

"I'm right behind you."

Rikki was coming out of the ICU as we stepped off the elevator.

"He's sleeping," she assured Becca.

"Good," the redhead responded.

"Do you need anything?" Rikki asked.

Becca shook her head. "Your dad's business manager... Jackson, I think... has arranged a house for me to stay in."

"Yeah, Jackson should take care of you," Rikki offered in an awkward tone. "Call me though, if he or you need anything."

"Please, tell your dad thank you," Becca said.

Rikki nodded as she started toward the elevator.

"Thank you for the coffee, Chase."

"My pleasure," I returned as I followed Rikki through the elevator doors.

The elevator's motor whirred as we descended to the lobby.

"I did a quick search while Sam was resting," Rikki commented. "I think I know where to find Milo Oder."

"Can he help us?"

"I called him, and he thinks he can," she replied. "He's waiting on us."

"Miami?"

She nodded, "Miami."

13

Milo Oder lived in a lighthouse just south of Miami. The coastline had changed after Hurricane Andrew, and the lighthouse was no longer in navigable water except for small fishing boats and kayaks. The beacon was listed on a website for historical lighthouses of Florida. However, there was a note that it was now private property and the owner prosecuted all trespassers.

I felt like I'd spent more time on the road recently than I'd clocked in the last few years combined. My interest was waning as my legs cramped after four hours on Highway One.

Rikki seemed to have come out of her shell after visiting with Sam. She bubbled the entire ride, talking about the sights and growing up with Sam. Since we met, she had remained calm and collected during everything. This was a new level of energy that she was exhibiting. A mixture of anticipation and excitement. Perhaps knowing that Sam was going to recover was enough to launch her spirit.

"Who is Milo Oder?" I asked during one of her few seconds of silence.

"I didn't get much from Sam, obviously. But, he said he trusted him."

"Good," I commented. "What's Sam's story?"

"He's worked for my dad for as long as I can remember. Even before Mom died. He was in the military in Ireland when he was younger."

"He had to be tough to handle the beating he got."

"Oh, he is. That's how he met my dad. He was working on one of his movies, as a consultant. I think Dad hired him at first just to be his trainer. Benjamin Dexter had to look like a badass."

There were a lot of former military guys signing up as Hollywood consultants. The pay tends to far outweigh what the government paid.

Rikki continued, "They became close, and Dad offered him a permanent job."

"Is that it?" I asked.

"Yeah."

A stone structure rose up ahead of us. It was a magnificent building, stirring a sense of adventure for many. Behind the beacon, a solar array aiming to the south was a disparaging dichotomy–the future and the past merged.

A wrought-iron fence surrounding the tower stood 12 feet tall and posed a formidable challenge to intruders. To the east, the marsh that had once been a channel a hundred years ago, now functioned as a natural barrier that was likely home to a fair share of gators, acting as sentries for Oder's home.

"He is expecting us?" I double-checked.

Rikki nodded as she pulled up to a gate.

The speaker on the gate chirped when she pushed the button. A small camera mounted on top stared into the Jeep. There were at least three other cameras visible. Each mounted on the black-iron fence.

"Yes?" came the response.

"Rikki Talen for Milo Oder," she spoke to the microphone.

The magnetic lock on the gate made a loud click as it released its hold. The metal arm retracted as the gate swung open.

"Pull through," the voice ordered in a British accent.

Rikki drove up the driveway to a small parking area. A covered carport housed a vintage silver Aston Martin. The Jeep stopped behind the carport.

"There's the front door," Rikki pointed.

"Is it?" I questioned. "It's a round building. How do we know which way is the front?"

She rolled her eyes at me with a smirk. Before she could comment, the door in question opened. A tall thin gentleman in his 60s stepped onto the small wooden porch.

"Greetings," he offered.

"Mr. Oder?" Rikki asked.

"Please," he stopped her. "Milo."

I extended my hand, "I'm Chase. This is Rikki."

"Oh, I know who Rikki is." His mouth widened in a broad grin. He added, "Sam's talked about you many times."

A confused look crossed her face before she shook it off and took his hand. "It's nice to meet you."

"From your call, I gather Sam is doing better."

She nodded. "Better is subjective though. He has a lot of recovery to do."

"If anyone is tough enough, it's that bastard," he chuckled. "Why don't you come inside?"

As Oder led us into his home, Rikki asked, "How do you know, Sam?"

The inside of the lighthouse could have been a library at Harvard or Yale. Dark-stained wooden shelves lined the walls. Books filled up every slot on the shelves. A leather sofa sat opposite two high-back chairs that had the aura of high-dollar antiques. Not that I'm much of an expert on furniture.

He motioned for us to take a seat on the sofa as he chose one of the chairs.

"That's a long story," he began, "that dates back to the '70s. I was working for MI-5 at the time."

"Sam was in MI-5?"

"No, dear, and those are stories best left for Sam to share with you," he explained. "Suffice it to say, Sam Cornell is one of my most trusted comrades."

My eyes examined the older man. "Why would he suggest we come to you?" I asked him.

"I can't say," Oder stated. "However, I would guess he thinks my collection of knowledge might assist you."

As he spoke, his hand waved about the room.

"Books?" Rikki pondered.

"Yes, dear." He continued, "Quite an extensive collection of them. One of my loves has always been research. This began while I was working for MI-5 when I just began picking up works for intelligence gathering. Soon it became something of an obsession. History fascinated me, and I developed an addiction."

Rikki exchanged a glance with me. I shrugged.

"This started with a rumor of some gold that the Nazis might have lost."

Oder grinned. "Nazi gold. That's always exciting. I think there is a great deal of Nazi treasures still lost out there in the world."

Rikki stated, "This was just a little string I wanted to tug on. I never expected it to go anywhere, certainly not this fast. Things got a little heated when men killed my captain and nearly killed Sam. Then, they tried to kidnap me."

Oder listened, asking, "And you think it relates to your gold?"

My hand raised to interject. "The men had Swastika tattoos. It seemed like a reasonable conclusion."

"Indeed," he agreed. "What have you found so far?"

Rikki began explaining her theory. How she thought Germany might have sent a U-boat to Cuba with a substantial payment to ensure an alliance with the island country.

"Very possible," Oder agreed. "The backing of Cuba would help hold the Gulf of Mexico, and with Germany as an ally, Cuba could have blossomed. Of course, all of that hinged on Germany winning the war, but at the time, we have to assume that Hitler thought he could."

"It could have coincided with an attempt to kidnap Edward."

Oder brightened. "I might have just the thing," he howled with excitement.

He bounded out of his seat. "Come with me," he ordered.

We were right behind him as he began ascending a narrow staircase.

"I'm certain it's on the third level," he blurted out as he skipped up the stairs.

The third floor of the lighthouse held rows of shelves. Like the ones in Oder's study, they were packed full of books, papers, and folders.

"Rusty Adams," Oder mumbled to himself. "That's who you want."

"Who is Rusty Adams?" Rikki asked as Oder began traipsing down the rows of books.

"Russell Adams. He was an operative for the O.S.S." He paused as he scanned a shelf. "The Office of Strategic Services was the precursor to your C.I.A."

"What did Russell Adams do?" I reworded Rikki's question.

"In short," Oder answered, "he was a Nazi hunter."

My head cocked to the side, and I raised an eyebrow. "Nazi hunter? Wouldn't that have been the entirety of the American military back then?"

Oder smiled in my direction. "Well, there was the Pacific theater."

I sighed, and Oder chuckled to himself. "While the war waged in Europe, Rusty Adams was more like a scalpel, cutting away cancerous cells. The SS attempted to weave its grasp into all areas of the world. The OSS tasked Adams with finding and stopping that reach. He was more than a little effective doing it."

"Aha," he exclaimed as he climbed up on the bottom shelf and reached up to grab a leather-bound journal. "Here it is."

"What?"

"The journal of Colonel Russell Adams," he said, holding the book aloft with a prideful smile.

"Come," he demanded. "This will deserve a good cup of tea before we delve into it."

The lanky Brit bounced down the stone steps, leading us into a quaint kitchen. The stainless-steel appliances were designed to have a vintage facade, but they were new energy-saver models.

Oder filled a kettle with water and put it on the eye of the stove. Next, he put three Delft blue porcelain cups on the round kitchen table.

"Adams kept a meticulous journal of all his missions. The damned things read like an Ian Fleming novel, which is à propos given that he was the Yanks real-life equivalent at the time."

He motioned for us to take a seat, and he chose the one closest to the stove. "Many of his writings were official reports, and they floundered in some file cabinet labeled 'Top Secret' for decades. A few floated around. Adams had a tendency to stash a journal while he was on a mission, in case he was killed. The problem with that being that since he was often off-the-books and undercover, he spread those around the world like the apple seeds of your proverbial Johnny Appleseed.

"This one, I received as a bit of quid pro quo. The journal had already been scanned and digitized, and the physical copy was simply taking up space."

The kettle whistled, and Oder retrieved it. "Sorry, I just have tea," he apologized.

"Tea is fine," I assured him.

He poured the steaming water into my cup. "Recon?" he asked, gesturing to my tattoo.

"Yes, but I've been out a few years now."

"You'd like Rusty then," he joked, referring to Adams by his nickname. "He began his career as a Marine too. A Raider. Before the government recruited him into the O.S.S. He joined up in '38, if I remember correctly."

"You almost seem like a fanboy," I kidded him.

Oder laughed, "I suppose. But, in truth, I would like to document his adventures. Write a complete biography on the man. I don't have quite enough of his journals though."

He sat back down and flipped through the leather book. "Here we go," he started.

14

December 12, 1940

I've counted five of them. Two women and three men.

I am not aware whether the Governor or any of his staff have any collusion with the men. The Duchess makes regular forays from the Government House with a small court of women, guarded by two Royal guards.

The concierge of the Whyte Conch Hotel informed me that the Duchess has coffee at their cafe every Monday and Thursday. She often has a companion but will dine alone.

One of the two women from the group made contact with the Duchess last Thursday while she was alone in the cafe. The encounter could have been planned, but from the outside, it appeared to be coincidental. A brief conversation occurred where the two seemed to exchange pleasantries before the Duchess offered the woman a seat. I remained at a distance and, as such, was unable to hear their conversation. It appeared to be light-hearted and jovial, leading me to assume that the Duchess was unaware that the woman was a Nazi.

When the two finished their tea, I was able to follow the woman. Fortunately, she was unaware of my presence, and she led me to a small apartment, where I was able to identify the other four members of their unit.

The leader is a young man in his 30s, although I suspect that his youthfulness is part of his disguise. The other two men bore bolder features. Both are taller and broader than the leader. They have piercing eyes. They don't leave the apartment often, and, even then, the trips are short.

Yesterday, the leader visited the Government House, where he milled around and chatted up some guards. I waited until he had left before approaching one of the men with which he spoke. Under the guise of one of the Governor's staff, I questioned the driver about the man.

When I spoke to the driver, the man stated that he was visiting from Suffolk and had great admiration for the Duke. He wondered if there would be any public addresses by the Governor. He continued to offer his admiration for the Governor, stating that he never had a chance to see him in person while he was the King. It would be such a pleasure to hear the man speak.

The driver didn't seem to be a cohort of the unit, but instead an unsuspecting pawn. However, he informed the unit's leader that there was a ceremony in three days where the Governor would be attending.

The event wasn't considered secretive, and the driver meant no harm in discussing it.

December 13, 1940

One of the other two men left the apartment alone. I followed him. He appeared to be going to the fish market.

It was time to disrupt the group's plans. I waited until he was taking an alley toward his apartment.

"Excuse me." I came up behind him.

He turned toward me, and brandishing my little rapier blade, I drove the knife toward him. He reacted quicker than I expected, tossing the wrapped fish at my hand. The raw seafood caught the point of my knife and ripped it out of my hands.

The man outweighed me by at least 30 pounds. I was ready for him. He threw a balled up fist at my face, and I dodged it with ease. As I went under his arm, my hands could deliver three or four quick jabs into his kidneys. He was only somewhat fazed by the blows and countered with an elbow into my temple.

Stunned, I stepped back to get my bearings. He lunged at me, putting the force of his weight into the attack. I twisted away and drove my right foot into his groin. The kick stopped him as he doubled over. My arm wrapped around his neck, wrenching until the bones connecting his skull to his spine broke in my grip.

We were still alone in the alley, and I made haste in searching the body. The man only had a few pounds on him—no other identification. With considerable effort, I dragged his body to an empty trash bin, hoping I had a couple of days before someone discovered his body. To ensure that, I gathered some refuse in the street and piled it on top of the corpse.

December 14, 1940

The four remaining members of the unit have been holed up in their apartment since last night. I've been able to rent a room across the street from them. If they intend to make a move against the Governor tomorrow, I expect they will be forced to make arrangements.

The missing man may be giving them pause, and I hope that they'll make a mistake.

2:45 pm

The woman I had seen with the Duchess at the Whyte Conch exited the rear entrance for the building. Naturally, I anticipated such an action, ensuring that I had a view of the alleyway.

The woman was easy to follow. She was blond, tall, and very handsome. She was wearing a simple dress and pulled her hair back. A fruitless attempt to blend with the crowd; she would stand out on any street, much less one in Nassau.

I've employed Mickey, a local young man, to keep an eye on the apartment when I'm not around. He has proven very adept at surveillance, and he knows the city.

With Mickey in place, I pursued the woman, who led me through the straw market. I suspected she was a ploy to discover the presence of enemy agents. It took a few minutes, but I was able to locate the other man from her unit. He was of a similar size to the man I dispatched in the alley.

As I weaved through the stalls and stands selling woven baskets and fruit, the woman I trailed made a mistake. She paused at a stall and examined the fruit available. I slipped into a booth down from where she was shopping. The vendor greeted me, and I passed her a few coins as I exited out the back of her stall.

Out of sight of either of the two agents, I was able to move behind the man, who was lurking behind a stand offering seedlings and full-sized vegetable plants. He was intent on the booth I had disappeared into.

He was attempting to remain hidden from the main thoroughfare. The silver dagger slipped from its sheath on my forearm as I stepped up behind him and cut his throat. He gurgled as he collapsed. As he dropped, I caught his weight and lowered him to the ground. Without the benefit of privacy, I moved with diligence to drag him out of sight.

His body would be discovered soon. Time was of the essence. I moved back behind the kiosks as I re-sheathed the blade and emerged on the other side of the woman. She had moved down a few more stands, but she was taking quick glances back, looking for her compatriot or me.

When she saw neither of us, she gathered her resolve and turned to make a hasty retreat, likely assuming that her partner had taken me out of the way.

As she passed my hiding place, I stepped up behind her and caught her right arm, with the barrel of my Colt 1903 into her ribs.

"Stay calm," I ordered her.

"What are you doing?" she exclaimed. She tried to cover her accent, and the words sounded stifled.

"We are going to have a talk," I explained. "If you make a scene, I'll shoot you and disappear."

She looked back for her partner.

"He's not going to help you," I assured her, and her face looked down.

We marched through the back streets until we arrived at my room. I stayed behind her as I escorted her upstairs to my room, where I forced her to sit in the wooden chair. After tying her legs to the chair and binding her hands, I made sure that she couldn't attempt to make an escape.

"I want to know what your plan is."

She shook her head. "I don't know what you are talking about, Mister," she insisted. Her American accent sounded flawless now.

With a scowl, I stared at her. "I don't have time for this," I told her. "I expect that in a few hours your friends will get nervous when the two of you don't return. What are they going to do?"

Her blue eyes blinked.

"There's only two left," I pointed out. "Can they pull off whatever the plan is with just two?"

"What are you talking about?" she repeated.

I whipped the silver blade off my arm with a resolute sigh. "I don't like hurting women," I sighed. "Don't force me to make an exception."

She flinched as the blade came close to her face. Her eyes narrowed as they followed the point of the dagger.

"Please," she begged. The German accent bled through as the fear overwhelmed her.

"What's the plan?"

"We were supposed to grab the Duchess," she admitted. "Adette, the other girl, was going to take her place and get close enough to the Duke. She has similar features."

"Will they be able to do it with only two?"

She shook her head. "I don't think so."

"Are there any reinforcements? Any other agents in the islands?"

She blinked twice. "Not nearby."

"What was the plan once you had the Duke?"

"We were to take a boat to rendezvous at Darby Island."

"Rendezvous with whom?"

"A submarine is to meet us there. I don't know the details. Emery is in charge of that. He has been arranging the meet."

"What happens if Emery isn't there?"

She shrugged.

"You get lucky," I informed her. "If you stay put, then you get to live out a long life."

She stared at me.

"Or at least a longer life than if you don't."

Her eyes watered, but she tried to display her German stoicism. After tightening her binds, I gagged her and pushed her chair into a corner.

With only two of their team remaining, I decided to eliminate Emery. If the women weren't a problem, then I'd leave them alive. I suspected this one was an amateur. She could have been an actress. However, something about her demeanor told me she wasn't a hardened asset.

After crossing the street, I entered the building where the others were hiding. It hadn't been too long since their team members left, and I hoped they weren't suspicious yet.

The apartment was on the second floor. With only three doors to choose from, it was easy to decipher which would have been theirs. The door was locked. My Colt rested in the palm of my right hand.

My fist banged on the door as I shouted in German, "I'm back."

The door clicked as the locks were unlatched. As it swung open, I raised the Colt level with Adette's face. Her eyes widened, and I hit her between the eyes. The blow was enough to knock her out, but she should wake up unharmed.

Emery heard the ruckus as Adette fell to the floor. He barreled through a door as the Colt fired. The Nazi fell back as the bullet left him faceless.

After locking the door, I dragged Adette to the bed, where I tied her feet and hands like a newborn calf. A search of the room provided very little—falsified documents for all five of them. I took them all. The women might find it difficult getting off the island without identification. The only thing I found was a map of the islands. A penciled line dotted between the city of Nassau and a nameless island to the south. The tiny island was circled. Darby Island?

December 15, 1940

After finding the boat I believe Emery had acquired, I have determined the location of Darby Island as the one circled on the map. I am mailing my journal to Washington before provisioning for the several day journey to investigate Darby Island.

The local authorities are searching for the killer of the two men I dispatched in the city. Emery's body hasn't been discovered yet, and the two women are still tied up. They could be a loose end; however, I don't feel justified in removing them at the moment.

15

"That's the end of that journal," Oder commented as he closed the leather-bound book.

"We don't know for certain that the sub he was chasing is the same one we are," Rikki pointed out.

My eyes fixated on a painting in the other room. A two foot by three-foot oil painting of the surf pounding against the rocks. The journal entry was engaging. With a bit more detail throughout the report, it would make quite an adventure novel.

"When did the Altmans pull Richman out of the water?" I asked, still staring at the white-tipped waves.

"January 3rd."

"19 days after Adams's last entry."

Rikki nodded.

Oder stood up and vanished into the other room. He returned a minute later with a rolled up chart and a ruler. He weighted down the two opposite corners with the sugar caddy and cream container and spread the chart out on the table.

With a stubby pencil, he circled Nassau on the island of New Providence. He connected New Providence to a small island, tracing a straight line south against the ruler.

"That's close to 170 kilometers," he pointed out after measuring the route. "It would take him about two days to make the journey, if he powered through. But, of course, that would depend on how fast the boat he had was."

"Give him three days," I suggested. "He made it to Darby Island by December 18. Even if he made a stop or two along the way, he would arrive by the 20th."

Rikki perked up, saying, "Jacob said the man had been in the water a few days too."

"They could set sail any day around the end of December," I observed.

Oder seemed to revel in our theorizing. A wry grin molded around his mouth. His eyes tracked along the pencil route to Darby Island.

"Were there any other reports from Adams?" I asked the former spy, interrupting his mental processes.

"Not that I possess," he assured me. "Although, I'm sure some exist. Adams died an old man, so he survived whatever came next."

Rikki looked at me. "Whatever we are going to find next is going to be there." Her finger pressed on the small island. "We are going to Darby Island."

Oder's eyes twisted off in thought. He seemed to search for some invisible object in the air as he mumbled, almost to himself, "Darby Island. There's something on the edge of my brain about that place."

His head shook in frustration as he tried to grasp the tidbit of information from the ether. When he glanced our way and realized we were both staring at him, his face displayed a sheepish mask.

"I'm sorry," he apologized. "I have an eidetic memory, but my brain misfiles it all the time. Wait, I got it."

The old man pounced off his seat and scampered out of the room like a kid chasing a puppy.

"Do we follow him?" I asked Rikki as the man's footsteps pounded up the wooden staircase.

"I doubt we can keep up," she pointed out. "Besides, we'd get lost in the maze of books." Rikki leaned over the chart and traced her finger on a path from Key West to the circled dot of green Darby Island. "I don't suppose we could fly in. You said you knew how to fly."

A chuckle erupted from my chest as I shook my head. "I think not. It doesn't look like there's any place to land. We don't know the terrain well enough."

"Besides," I added, "what I said was that I used to fly. Without a license, much less a plane, I don't think it's an option."

"A plane wouldn't be a problem. We could get one," Rikki commented.

In disbelief, I responded, "Not one I plan to fly."

Her next remark was an off-color stab at my masculinity, which wasn't affected by her jab.

"How long would it take to get there in *Talitha*?" she asked, after giving up the idea of flying.

With the ruler lying on the corner of the table, I studied the map, following a route from Key West north. Once I created a course, I started counting the miles.

My back straightened as I examined the map. "That's about 500 miles. It'd take 25 to 30 hours non-stop, assuming we can hold a steady 20 knots. Plus, we'd lose a day just checking into the country."

"We couldn't skip that?" she questioned.

"No," I stated with a vigorous head shake. "I plan to make several more trips there, and I have no intention of being flagged by the Bahamian government."

Rikki sighed in a loud protest.

"We can't make that trip non-stop either," I pointed out. "Break those 30 hours into about 4 days."

"Ugh," she groaned. "We need to get there."

"You need to find some patience," I urged. "Besides, you don't have a captain, and your boat is in police custody at the moment."

"You're a captain," she commented.

"No, I'm not," I refuted. "I can drive a boat, but I'm only a captain of my boat."

"Come on," she insisted. "We can do it. It'll be an adventure. What if we find the gold there?"

"It would take us longer," I pointed out. "We couldn't go straight through."

The corners of her mouth turned up. "You said four days."

"If we had a captain," I amended.

"Come on, it'll be fun," she promised.

The moment her nose crinkled with her smile, I knew I had given in.

"The only way we can do it is if you get your boat out of the police's possession."

Her mouth widened in a smile, and she swept in and kissed me. It was meant as a quick peck, but it lasted a second longer than that. Her lips tasted like salt and lime, and I closed my eyes and inhaled.

"Found it," Oder announced as he bounded back into the room.

We both straightened up as he spoke. "Darby Island was gifted to Sir Guy Baxter by King George. Baxter vanished sometime in the 1940s–disappeared during the war. He was suspected of being a Nazi sympathizer, and local legends state that the neighboring residents ran him off."

Oder added, "He reportedly maintained a network of caves as a docking station for submarines."

"What else did you find out?" Rikki asked, her voice brimming with elation. Her face beamed.

"There's not much about him," Oder admitted. "I can do some digging with some mates in London, but I only have a rumor written up in a New Providence newspaper in 1952."

"He's a ghost, huh?" I commented.

"Seems so," Oder admitted. "He turned Darby Island into a successful plantation, but then he was just gone."

We sat in silence for a minute. Finally, Oder broke the quiet, saying, "If you are chasing submarines, it seems Rusty Adams might bring you here." His finger touched the circled island.

Rikki stood up. "Let me make a phone call," she announced before walking outside.

Oder and I stared at each other.

"Recon, huh? Did you work with General Shaw?"

My eyebrow cocked with curiosity as I responded, "She was my CO."

"Hell of a woman." He grinned with some lascivious memories.

"I can't say to that," I commented. "She was a hell of a commanding officer. Did she give me a good recommendation?"

Oder's eyes twinkled when he laughed. "You're a quick one."

"What?" I asked. "Did you put in a call while you were out of the room?"

He nodded.

"You two must be close," I pointed out. "She rarely answers on the first ring."

Oder laughed again. "She didn't say you were that quick, though."

I shrugged.

Oder continued, "Judi said you were hell on wheels, but that you'd do what you were supposed to do."

"Just aim and shoot," I told him.

"I think it was, 'Point him where you want him to go, and stand out of the way.'"

"Be sure to thank her for the confidence when you talk to her again."

"Your friend?" he halfway asked.

"We haven't known each other long," I informed him. "She seems to be capable. She's handled two of the men that attacked us without batting an eye."

"If Sam had anything to do with her training, I expect she's damn near-deadly."

"You trust Sam?" I questioned.

Oder nodded. "Sam is one of the most honorable men I've come up against."

"Ah," I realized aloud. "Sam was IRA?"

Oder waved off the question. "Not my story to tell," he countered. "Needless to say, the man is a trusted friend."

"Is this the point where you warn me to make sure nothing happens to her? You and Sam might take it as a personal affront?"

Oder studied me. "In my prime, that would have been a threat," he assured me.

"I don't doubt it one bit," I agreed. "Just so you know, she's the one dragging me along, but I promise to do my best to protect her."

The wooden outside door opened, and Rikki came back inside. "I just got off the phone with my lawyer. We should be able to leave on *Talitha* in the morning."

"I'd suggest we get going to pack, but everything I have right now is on my back."

Rikki offered Oder a card. "It's my number," she explained. "If you find anything else about Rusty Adams, please let us know."

16

It took two days before we could depart. Usually when I decide to cross the Gulf Stream for the Bahamas, I spend weeks prepping *Carina*. There are over 700 islands and 2,000 cays populating the Bahamas. Some are remote and uninhabited.

Those are the ones I search for. Places where the tourists don't swarm. Places where I can't hear the television on the next boat.

More than one person has told me I'm anti-social, which is far from the truth. After years of living with a constantly revolving band of other Marines, I value quiet anchorages where I can get to know myself.

Those remote anchorages mean that anything I needed would have to be brought with me, stored somewhere aboard *Carina*. Food, drink, boat parts, or anything else were stuffed into cabinets, cubbyholes, and confines. There weren't always boat-yards nearby, and repairs would fall to me alone. And those supplies would need to last me two to three months. So there wouldn't be a bit of extra space in my storage lockers when I set off from the dock.

Of course, this wasn't a multi-month trip. But it wasn't a weekend trip either. A week to get to Darby Island and a week back. Who knows how long in between?

Rikki's lawyer spent the better part of a day arguing with the Monroe County Sheriff's Department, and in particular, Detective Cooper, that the *Talitha* was Rikki's home, and as such she needed to be allowed back on board. The rest of the time was a legal debate over whether she was required to stay in the state. If there were no charges brought against Rikki or myself, there was no justification for preventing us from traveling.

While all the legal ramifications were being dealt with, Rikki and I worked to gather any provisions we would need. If we found our quarry, it would likely be at the bottom of the ocean somewhere. We wanted plenty of scuba equipment and salvage gear. If there was even a second's thought that something might be needed, we gathered it.

Underwater salvage wasn't in my wheelhouse, but the Corps did see fit to train me in aquatic rescue and demolition. The principles might vary somewhat, but the general practice was close enough.

Talitha had a davit on the stern for lifting a tender. With a longer cable and a metal platform, the davit would create an ideal lift for thousands of pounds of gold. When I was finished modifying the lifts, an eight by eight platform could be lowered as deep as 400 feet. However, if we were forced to go that deep, we were going to need different equipment. I could handle salvaging anything as deep as

150 feet. But, unfortunately, I wouldn't be able to stay at that depth too long.

Once loaded and released, we pointed the bow of the Nomad yacht north toward Bimini, where we checked in with the Bahamian government.

From the bridge, I maneuvered *Talitha* into a small cove. Since leaving the marina yesterday, we covered almost 300 nautical miles. The autopilot helped during the long stretches, but one of us was forced to maintain a watch. We stayed in Bimini for a total of six hours, just long enough to clear the quarantine period and check in.

If we stayed still too long, Richman or his Nazi goons would have a better chance to find us. As long as we were off-grid, we stood a good chance of staying out of their crosshairs.

That just meant that now I was beat. I loved being at the helm of pretty much any boat, but despite the allure and beauty of the vast blue seas, it can be tiring. I was dreaming about a quick sandwich and a solid eight hours in the sack.

After I checked the depth gauge, I released the controls for the anchor windlass. The vibrations of the chain grinding out of the anchor locker could be felt through the hull. The water along the western coast of Andros Island was crystal clear. The white, sandy, shallow ocean floor is what offers such pale blue waters around these islands.

The water was about 16 feet deep, and I watched the counter on the windlass control click past 25 feet. Slowly, I pulled the throttle in reverse, allowing the needle of the tachometer to wiggle around 1,000 RPM. This would dig the plow anchor firmly into the sand.

Once I was satisfied that the anchor was set, I released another 175 feet of chain. After that, we could rest easy, making a big arc around the 85 pound anchor.

The green island sat off the starboard bow. My back rested against the seat as I took a moment to soak in the view. Andros Island is the largest of all the Bahamian islands. In fact, it is larger than all the islands combined. Yet, with a population of less than 8,000, it seems almost deserted. During my first trip on *Carina*, I spent two months circling the island. The mixture of lush inland greenery and perfect diving conditions made it a veritable paradise. The few people that did make their home on this chunk of heaven were some of the most delightful and friendly folks I'd ever met.

This was just a stopping off point, though. No time to snorkel the "blue holes" that cover the island. These pockets of crystal clear water are openings into the vast underwater cave system that Swiss-cheeses its way beneath the paradise. Those adventures would have to wait for another day.

Rikki had been below deck for the last few hours, and now that we were securely hooked, I decided to go below and find her and the tuna sandwich I had been thinking about.

The galley was less than ship-shape. Rikki was plating up a pile of noodles. She'd donned a simple white sun-dress that hung off her shoulders with two small straps.

"Hey," she greeted me as I came down the steps. "I almost had this done in time."

The table had been set with wine glasses and silverware. "What's all this?"

She smiled. "My attempt at domesticity."

"Domesticity?" I repeated. "That doesn't seem to fit you at all."

"Well, I know how to make one thing well. Noodles. Luckily, I can add a jar of spaghetti sauce and some shrimp. It makes it seem gourmet."

"You shouldn't tell all your secrets," I suggested as I sat down at the table.

The bottle of wine rested in what had been a small piece of driftwood. The center had been carved into a circle, perfectly sized for the average bottle of wine. It was a unique design that could prevent the bottle from sliding or tipping with the gentle rocking of the hull. My hand pulled the Cabernet from its holder, and I began opening the bottle with the corkscrew on the table.

"Somehow, I bet that you already figured that out about me," she purred.

The cork popped loudly. Despite a few years behind the bar, my expertise in wine is limited. I can, however, recognize a label or two. This one was a 2015 Chateau Lafitte Rothschild Cabernet, and while I couldn't guess its value, I knew it was going to be one of the most expensive drinks I'd ever consumed.

"Might want to let it breathe a minute," I suggested.

"Absolutely," she responded in a giddy voice.

She bounced about the galley, moving from the sink to the stove in quick, excited steps. It wasn't something I would have noticed, except that it was a stark contrast from the woman I'd spent the past few days getting to know. Rikki was full of life. I saw that the first moment I laid eyes on her, coasting up to shore on the kite board. This was different, though. She was cooking dinner for me, and it wasn't the same joy.

This was different, and, without sounding too egotistical, I knew what it meant. We were about to shift the dynamics around, and I would have lied if I said the thought hadn't occurred to me.

She placed a plate filled with spaghetti noodles, tomato sauce, and bright pink shrimp the size of a healthy bratwurst before me. Sprinkles of grated cheese and fresh basil covered the top.

"The basil is what makes it gourmet," she informed me. "Think you can pour the wine now?"

Obliging, I filled the large, round, crystal glasses just past the curve of the glass. She lifted her wine, and I clinked the crystal together. The ding hung in the air for a second as I took in the beaming face across from me.

"Thank you," I offered. "I wasn't expecting this."

"I'm the one that should be thanking you," she explained. "You've jumped on this insane trip without a thought. I wouldn't be this close without you."

I shrugged.

"Besides," she added, pausing as she took a long sip. "I wasn't sure if you'd actually make a move or not."

I almost snorted mid-sip. Rikki's dark brown eyes stared over the rim of her glass at me.

"I promise you a move would have been made," I assured her.

"Really?" she gasped with fake shock, "you've had ample time."

Her chair scraped the deck as she pushed away from the table. Rikki set her glass down and rose to her feet. "I think the wine needs to breathe a bit longer," she said.

"But our food might get cold," I pointed out as she pulled me up from my seat.

"This is a first-class yacht," she apprised me. "We have a fully functional microwave."

My fingers ran up her arm and along her neck until I cradled her cheek in the palm of my hand. Her eyes grew wider, and she kept them locked on mine. Her hand entwined in my hair and pulled my face toward her.

Our mouths connected as I lifted her off the ground. Her arms wrapped around my shoulders as I stumbled back into the lounge area. For a split second, I felt the eyes of Moses Carter staring down at me. The second was gone as I dropped back onto the couch and Rikki pulled back for a second. Her pupils widened as she shifted her weight on my lap.

When my hands traced the curve of her thigh, they slid under the soft cotton dress toward her hips. Her skin was silk, and as I slipped the dress over her head, she pressed against me, kissing me as she pushed me back.

17

Her lips on my neck woke me up. The sun was streaming through the curtains in the master cabin, silhouetting Rikki's head. She shifted, blocking the rays of light. Her dark brown eyes leered at me with some anticipation.

"Morning," she whispered.

"Looks like we are well into the morning," I pointed out, judging by the sun's position in the middle of the eastern sky.

"You had a late night." Her mouth widened into a broad smile.

My arm wrapped around her back and pulled her toward me. My lips caught hers, and I rolled her over.

When I raised up, I lifted the right side of my mouth in a smirk. "We don't have time for that," I informed her.

She pouted, pursing her lips in protest.

"It's your treasure hunt," I remarked.

"I know," she huffed, "I've just enjoyed the past few days."

With a relaxing sigh, I had to agree. The past three days had been a blur as we continued toward Darby Island. The nights were filled with stars, wine, and each other. We moved from unbridled passion to learning about each other's movements. The tingle of each kiss, the electricity of every caress, the soulful gazes across the deck blended into euphoria.

"Imagine," I offered, "a repeat of those last three days, only this time, we have your trove of racist gold."

Her grin reappeared. "You sure know how to make a girl swoon."

"It's all part of the training."

She kissed me again as her fingers traced down my stomach. "How good is your training?" she rasped between kisses.

My arms pushed her off me as I muttered, "Limited to resistance to torture only."

She started cackling as I twisted around and dropped my bare feet to the carpeted floor. The comfort level in a super yacht like *Talitha* outweighed what *Carina* offered. My 40-foot Tartan sailboat was more compact. I didn't have multiple decks to spread out my living space. Instead, everything was crammed into less than 300 square feet. *Talitha* had over four times the square footage. Which meant that when I woke up on board *Talitha*, I could put my feet on the floor. On *Carina*, I slept in the v-berth, which required some agility to get under the sheets.

Even the windows on the 65-foot floating castle shamed my poor little boat. The portholes on *Carina* were just that, holes. Talitha offered extensive, picturesque views from every deck. I stood naked in front of the window and stared at the rock wall looming a few hundred yards off the starboard bow.

Of course, I don't think I'd trade for a powerboat soon. There's still something about the tilt of a sailboat as it flies across the water with the sails filled with wind. The fuel costs alone for *Talitha* would keep me in beer and cheese for two months.

Talitha was anchored in 16 feet of water off the northern tip of Darby Island. From where I was standing, I could see the sandy bottom. Dark blobs were scattered along the sea floor, likely rocks that had tumbled from the island.

When we arrived yesterday afternoon, the wind was coming from the south. The cliff wall overlooking us protected us from the gusts, but even if the anchor didn't hold, the wind would blow us away from the rocky shore.

Rikki padded up beside me. "What are you thinking?" she asked.

As I glanced over at her, I commented, "I think we're going to be forced to go around the eastern edge of the island, unless we want to scale the walls."

"I have climbing gear," she told me.

"You're a climber too?"

"Oh yeah!" she exclaimed.

"What don't you do?"

She leaned into my ear and moaned, "Not much."

I cut my eyes to watch her walk past the bed to grab a shirt.

"Let's go explore a Nazi castle," she muttered as she slipped into the button-down shirt.

Darby Island is uninhabited. As we made our way, Rikki did some searching online about it. From satellite images, we found the only structure on the island is the former residence of Guy Baxter. Unfortunately, nature swallowed the only roads leading to the house over the last 80 years.

The tender bounced away from *Talitha*. From my position at the center console, I steered the 20-foot inflatable around the rocky point of Darby Island. The 250-horsepower outboard pushed us over the waves. As we wound our way around the island, the contour of the archipelago changed. The towering cliff sloped toward the sea. The rocks gave way to scrub brush. Only a few trees visible, and those that I could see were less than ten feet tall, having fallen victim to hurricane-force winds.

"I want to circle the island," I told her.

Oder told us that Guy Baxter allowed German U-boats to dock and take shore leave here. However, the water we anchored in was shallow, and I wasn't sure how deep a submarine would need to avoid grounding.

The island had over five miles of shoreline, and we spent an hour cruising along like regular sightseers. But, besides the slope from the cliffs to sea level, the land seemed flat. And lifeless. There were no signs of life, human or animal.

Even more disappointing was the lack of any sign of pier or pylon. A hundred yards from shore saw the depth vary some but stayed around 10 to 20 feet deep.

"Could there be an underwater entrance?" Rikki queried.

"Hard to say. We can't see it."

When we passed Talitha after making a complete circuit, I followed the cliff wall for about a quarter mile south before the rock wall staring down at the sea turned into a rocky beach. I steered the boat to land, angling the bow of the tender toward the shore.

"Be ready to catch us," I warned Rikki, who sat perched on the starboard rail.

She gave me an affirming nod and swung her feet over the side as I slowed the motor. She dropped off the inflated tube, landing in ten inches of water. Grabbing the painter attached to the bow of the dinghy, Rikki guided the hull between two medium-sized boulders while I lifted the motor to prevent the propeller from scraping the rocky bottom.

Each of us brought a backpack stocked with water and supplies. I tossed Rikki the green one she had packed. Her hand caught the strap and swung the pack over her other arm in one fluid motion. My arms slid through the straps of the other one as I jumped into the shallow surf. Together we heaved the boat higher on shore.

Up the incline, I noted a narrow path. Rikki took off, scrambling up the rocks. The sawgrass slapped our legs as we waded toward the house atop the island.

"Does kinda look like a castle," I commented.

"I thought it would be more like a plantation-style mansion."

The house that Sir Guy Baxter built was a smooth-faced, algae-colored building with round tower-like corners. It sat about half a mile ahead of us. The odd greenish color could have been a natural film, or the supposed Nazi could have lacked taste.

As I stared at the flat acreage stretching toward the house, I imagined fields of crops. "Didn't he have fields of sugar cane or something?"

"I think the internet said cotton."

"Seems about right," I muttered as I followed behind her.

Rikki was wearing a tan tank top and matching shorts. There was a brief discussion on whether long pants would be more appropriate, but as I didn't have a pair with me, I opted for my standard boat attire: a swimsuit and a light cotton shirt. The sea breeze countered the tropical sun, and my often overactive sweat glands kept their cool.

A half-opened, weather-worn mahogany door loomed at the center of the house. A covered portico wrapped around the house. Flakes of lime plaster had gone missing in places, exposing the reddish brick. Most of the storm shutters were missing, hanging, or decaying on the ground. Every window on the front was nothing more than shards of broken glass.

"I'm thinking summer home," I joked as we stepped up on the porch.

"You kid," Rikki commented, "but the structure itself looks intact for being abandoned for so long."

When I pushed the once ornate wooden door open, my hands felt across the splintering edges carved into the surface. The door swung wide with a menacing creak to reveal a dirty, white, marbled foyer. The interior walls had endured more damage over the years, most seemed to be the result of people. Vandals kicked holes into the walls. The crystal remnants of a chandelier were scattered on the floor.

As we moved into what looked to be a parlor, we stepped around broken furniture as we crossed the room. The picture window that offered a view of the blue water below was only a broken frame.

"It's been picked over," Rikki cursed.

"By tourists and, as my grandmother would have called them, 'lookie-loos.'"

"Your grandma sounds quaint."

I smiled. "Oh, she was from northern Arkansas. She'd hate you."

Rikki curled her lip. "Not a lot of brown people where you're from?"

My head shook as I admitted, "Not at all. I grew up in what would have been a sundowner county."

Her face twisted. It was a face I'd seen before. There was no excuse, no apology, and no amends can undo some atrocities. Even time, which seems like it would be the most effective avenue of change, has done nothing. Sundowner towns were still prevalent in the 80s, and while the bold signs warning Black people to stay away after nightfall had disappeared, the sentiment was saturated into the land.

Here we were, in the 21st century, still facing white supremacists, and time seems to have done little to change the attitude.

Rikki turned her attention to the stairs, a curving stone staircase that led up. "Those seem sturdy enough," she commented.

In the lead, I took my steps as close to the wall as possible. If the structure was going to fail, the joints on the wall would be the strongest.

The second floor mainly had minor damage. Intact pieces of furniture still stood in place after decades of neglect. The sun, wind, and rain that managed to get inside had done some damage, but the quality of the craftsmanship allowed the furnishings to survive.

We found a bedroom. The frame of the bed was broken beyond repair, but the dresser along the interior wall could have taken a heavy sanding and a coat of varnish to return it to near pristine condition.

"I doubt there's much in there," I stated, nodding toward the dresser, "but give it a look."

Rikki pulled open the drawers, one by one. Suddenly, on the third one, she jumped back as a mouse, startled by the sudden jolting of her home, scurried to carry three babies out the back of the drawer.

Before I could laugh, she scolded, "Don't. It just startled me."

I couldn't resist the smirk, though.

"What are we going to find here?" I asked.

"Evidence of a Nazi conspiracy," she offered.

"It's been over 80 years," I told her. "I don't think that any letters or books have survived this." My hands waved around the room at the time-ravaged state.

"If a submarine was here," she wondered, "where did it dock?"

I didn't have an answer. "It might be this is a dead end."

She sighed with frustration. Out of curiosity, we moved through the following four rooms upstairs. The only remnants of life here were the abandoned furniture.

"What if the treasure is neglected antiques? These pieces could bring several thousand if they were repaired."

"Not quite the same thrill of finding gold."

I shrugged. "Sometimes you gotta take what you can get."

Back on the first floor, we found our way back onto the portico. I hadn't noticed how stifling it was inside the castle until I felt the breeze on my clammy skin.

From the porch, I imagined what Guy Baxter must have seen in his day. This was paradise. The land still had the outlines where the earth had been tilled, or buildings had existed. The scars from only a few years of use were still clear 80 years later. East of the house was the ruin of a small stone structure. Maybe the larder or a shed.

My head turned toward Rikki as I asked, "If there was an underwater entrance for submarines, there would need to be access from above ground."

"Yes," she agreed, "but where?"

"Look at the ground," I told her. "Those lines in the dirt. The rocks. I bet it's the foundations of buildings. Over there could have been gardens."

She nodded. "And?"

"They're all close to the house."

Rikki wiped her forehead as she watched me.

"If you were Baxter, you'd want everything closer to the house. Even an entrance to your secret submarine dock."

"Wouldn't we see it?"

"I don't, so, I'm guessing the answer is, no, we wouldn't"

With a surge of vigor, Rikki marched off the porch. "You check that way," she commanded, pointing her finger east.

With the aid of small landmarks, like rocks and the corner of the house, I walked in a grid-like pattern, making each grid about 50 feet. If there was an entrance near the house, I guessed it would be large enough for a man to enter. Perhaps a natural opening.

"Chase!" Rikki shouted.

I jogged over and found her standing at the edge of the cliff, staring down at the sea.

"Do you see that?" she asked, aiming her finger down.

Beneath the rolling waves of crystal clear water, the ocean floor stretched out. White sand reflected the sun back up. The exception was the area where Rikki's attention was directed. A darker line came off the island and jutted out toward the deeper water.

Turning toward the center of the island, I imagined a continuation of the line. As I marched along my invisible path, I kicked a stone. The rock was carved into a small brick. The scrub brush had reclaimed the area, covering the piles of stone bricks.

By stomping the brush down with our feet, we started clearing the area until we found the crumbling foundation of the former brick wall. Broken bricks were cemented into the rocky terrain. The original builder had cut a shallow trench into the rock like a footing; the bricks lined the canal. As a testament to the builder, the footing and the remnants of masonry remained the only evidence of a structure.

Over the next half hour, we cleared the brush away by crushing it under our feet or pulling it free. Again, the shallow root system made it an easy, if not a quick, job.

The building had been rectangular. I paced off the edges, estimating it to be 60 feet long and 40 feet wide. The place where we guessed the door was located was marked by a three-foot gap in the trench. The entrance faced the house, only about 30 yards from the western corner. Rikki found another south-facing hole; this one was 10 feet wide, a double door for a cart or truck.

By examining the remains, it was clear the floor of the building was dirt and rock. As we brushed away the growth, we found the mortar lines of a bricked floor.

"Here," I directed Rikki. "This one's loose."

With a larger stone in my hand, I hammered it down on the loose brick. Two strikes broke the mortar free and cracked the clay brick. The broken chunks of red clay fell through the earth.

"Do you have a light?"

Rikki dug in the side pocket of her backpack and retrieved a small flashlight. Our faces lowered so we could peer down the hole. We could make out the edges of a shaft that turned into a deep black hole.

"We need some tools," she muttered.

When I glanced up at her, I saw the corners of her mouth turn up.

18

We stood over the hole we had created this morning. Once we found the passage was sealed, we spent a few minutes beating the bricks with other rocks. Our progress was exhausting, and after a few minutes, we realized that the prudent course would be to return to *Talitha* and find some more appropriate tools.

When dawn broke, we were already loading a couple of small sledge hammers and a hatchet stored in the yacht's engine room. The work moved fast as I pounded away at the bricks. Within two hours, the ground opened before us, and a dark shaft sank into the ground.

My legs straightened from where I had been squatting on the ground as I took in the breeze that cooled my sweaty skin. If I had a fedora, I would have donned it in a most adventurous manner as I stood over our excavation.

Rikki was pulling a coil of rope from her pack. We felt like the only people in the world, and from our vantage point, we could see a complete circle around the island.

There was not a boat, plane, or person in view. We might as well have been the last couple on Earth.

"Do you want me to go down first?" she asked, reiterating the plan we came up with last night.

"Yes," I confirmed. "I'll lower you, at least until you can drive a few pitons into the walls."

She laid out a couple of steel spikes with an eye on the end. As I let her down the shaft, Rikki would drive those pitons into the rock wall. Once they were secure, she could rappel down, leaving more pitons anchored on the way. Once she was down, I'd have to descend on my own.

Rikki drove a single piton into the ground and threaded her rope through it. With it secured to the piton, she dropped the remaining 200 feet of cord into the abyss. I wrapped my arm around the rope, gathering up some slack.

"Don't drop me," she ordered with a smile.

Her jest was just that. While anything like this has some risk, we were going down as safely as possible. My holding the line was only going to help her get the next couple of pitons driven into the wall.

She grabbed my cheeks in one of her hands and squeezed my face, puckering my lips. She kissed me through her laughter, took a step back, and dropped into the hole. The rope tightened around my arm, but the first spike she'd anchored held her weight.

Metal striking metal echoed out of the shaft. The rope twisted in my hand as Rikki moved around the cavern.

"One!" she shouted from underground.

More tinging as the hammer pounded against the next spike.

"Two!"

"Secure!" she informed me. "Let me go on three! One, two, three!"

The rope dropped from my hand as she pushed off the wall and released the grip on the brake she held in her hand. The slack in the line fell with her, and once she squeezed the brake, her descent stopped.

As I leaned over the opening, I saw she was resting with her feet against the wall as she pulled two more pitons off her belt. While the clanging persisted, I grabbed the other harness and slipped my feet through the leg holes. After cinching it tight around my waist, I checked the brake. Once Rikki made it to the bottom, I'd hook up to the same rope and start my descent.

The rope let out a twang, and I could tell she'd dropped again. I peered down the shaft again, but I could only see the light attached to her helmet. The camera was documenting everything as well as providing light. Once she found the bottom, she could retrieve the extra lights.

"You good?" I bellowed into the hole.

"Yes!" echoed up the chamber.

"Can you see anything?"

"I think there's something below me," she responded. "Another 30 feet or so."

The rope loosed for just under two seconds before it tightened again. A muffled voice came from below.

"What?" I shouted down the hole. The only thing I saw was dark. No glow from her camera.

"I'm down." It was a faint call. However, it was followed a few seconds later by a sharp jerk of the rope, a clear indication that she was unattached.

Once I was sure the rope would not come loose from my harness, I pulled up some slack until I had enough to hold one hand level with my chin and the other below my waist. Each palm was wrapped around a brake. The only thing left to do was take a small jump back and release the brake. Gravity would do the rest.

The blue skies, puffy clouds, and late morning sun rushed away as I fell back. The sensation of rappelling into the dark is like watching as the entire world vanishes. My heart fluttered as the adrenaline coursed through me. My feet caught the wall as I squeezed the brakes.

The soles of my shoes skipped off the wall as I launched back and dropped another 30 feet. I've descended plenty of mountains, buildings, and even from a chopper. The first drop hits me every time, and the rest of the descent has some calming effect. No matter how prepared or trained, the body doesn't understand the defiance of gravity.

Three times my feet bounced off the rocky wall before the shaft opened into an extensive black chamber. The air was chilly and damp. Water sloshed against stone somewhere and echoed throughout the dark.

"Almost there," Rikki called from the dark. Without the wall to catch me, I made quick stops every few feet to keep my drop slow.

A flash of light blinded me as her hand caught my arm. My foot touched solid ground, and I released the brakes.

"That was so much fun," she howled in the dark before kissing me.

"Exhilarating," I admitted as I started pulling the harness off. "Have you looked around?"

"Just a little," she answered. "There's the last of some wooden stairs that might have gone up the opening. Unfortunately, there's not much left of them."

Rikki waved a beam of light onto a woodpile, letting the circle of light crawl up the wall and circle around the room. Cables hung along the wall. Rusted shrouds that had once been lamps were attached to the cave wall. After retrieving a light from my pack, I scanned the other side of the cave.

"This place is huge," I confessed, amazed. "Gotta be 600 yards long."

"Look over here." Her light illuminated a pool of water. The black water was big enough to fit two boats as long as *Carina*.

"How deep do you think it is?" she asked.

"Enough for a sub," I answered. "There's no entry up here, so it must be below the surface."

"Charcoal," I commented, staring at burned timbers. "There was a fire down here."

"This has to be it," she mumbled to herself. Eventually, her light turned on me, and she started talking aloud. "This is where Rusty Adams was coming. It's where Henry Richman was."

"Could be," I conceded with some trepidation. "It's still speculation."

Rikki moved away from me. The cavern's blackness swallowed all of her, leaving only the beam of her light on a pile of wooden timbers and trash.

"Here." She knelt down and picked up something. When I reached her side, she held in her palm a small, corroded metal pin–an eagle with two S symbols underneath it.

"Let's assume that the Germans stopped here," I told her. "We still don't have any idea where they went from here."

"What about where Richman was found?" she questioned.

"But he was at sea for, who knows, how many days. I'd guess he was in a lifeboat and trying to make his way to America. I can't see him being able to hold on to a wooden box filled with gold if he was just bobbing along in the Gulf Stream. He had a chance to make a new life, and he took it. Where the Altmans rescued him won't help us much. We aren't sure how he got there."

She sighed. "You can sure take the steam out of a girl."

She couldn't see me smiling in the dark. I was about to make a lewd comment when something fell behind us.

"What was that?" Rikki asked, shining her light past me.

Turning, I saw the rope piled up on the cavern floor.

"Did that fall?"

With a quick glance over to Rikki, I furrowed my brow. "That shouldn't happen," I said.

I bent down and picked up the end to find a cut. "Shit!" I hissed.

Something echoed as it bounced off the walls above. Something small. The warning lights in my brain started flashing. Sirens screamed. All I could do was shout, "Run!"

The first grenade hit the ground and exploded. Rikki was in front of me, and the blast shoved me into her. The second bounced and rolled away before it exploded.

The boom echoed in the cavern, deafening us for a second. My left hand looped under her arm and lifted Rikki to her feet.

"Move!" I urged her.

The subsequent explosion was enormous. Whoever was up top timed a couple of grenade drops to blow at the same time. The concussion shoved us down, and I pushed her into the pool.

The water was far enough from the shaft that we only had to worry about falling debris, and the force from a few grenades would not be enough to bring down the cave.

When my head surfaced, I sucked in some air. Everything was black. The water splashing against the stone was the only thing I could hear.

"What the hell?" Rikki whispered.

"I'm guessing we had some company."

"How'd they find us?" she asked.

There were several ways, I reasoned, and some of them were worrisome. Oder was the only person we told where we were going, and I didn't think that he would cave under the kind of torture the guys we've met so far could mete out. If he told anyone, it was voluntary.

Richman might have heard of Darby Island. If his grandfather was on a submarine that stopped here, those stories might have been passed down.

"Doesn't matter," I told her. "They're not coming down here."

"What makes you say that?"

"Why cut the rope?" I pointed out. "Just slide down with guns a-blazing."

The cavern was quiet—no more explosions. I pulled myself up out of the water before offering my hand to Rikki.

"We need to find our lights," I told her.

"How are we going to get out of here?"

"I'm working on that."

Rikki found her helmet near the edge of the water. The light had fallen face down, giving only the faintest glow in the abyss. My light had still been in my hand when we hit the water, and I stared over the edge, attempting to see the beam in the depth below.

With the camera's light, Rikki found the other light. She had dropped it when I collided with her after the first blast.

"Does your phone have any signal down here?" I asked Rikki.

"It didn't, but that doesn't matter," she told me. "I dropped it when I fell in the water."

The beam flashed toward the shaft as she moved the light around, looking for another way out.

"We can't climb up there," she informed me.

As I studied the cavern, I realized she was right. Without getting up to the shaft opening, we couldn't climb out.

"How many pitons do you have left?" I asked her.

"Three."

Scaling the wall might be doable, but the ceiling would be impossible without the right equipment. Three pitons might get us across the ceiling if we had a way to anchor them. Free climbing to the top wasn't tricky. Hammering in a spike without being able to hold on to anything was another story.

"Can we build a scaffold out of anything?" I questioned.

Rikki swept the cave with her light. The burned timbers were too short to do much with. Even piled up, they wouldn't get us close to the shaft.

"How far up is the first piton?" I asked.

"Five to ten feet above the opening," she answered. "What, do you think you can lasso it?"

I shrugged, knowing full well the truth. I couldn't see it, and getting a rope around it would be pure luck.

"What about the water?" she asked. "It has to go somewhere."

"But we don't have a clue where or how far."

"The hole was only a few hundred feet to the cliff," she pointed out.

"But this cavern is bigger than that."

She let out a sigh. I paced the dark, thinking. They trapped us. If there was no other way out, the only exit might be the water. One had to admit drowning might be a faster demise than starving.

After walking along the edge of the entire cave, I found no cracks, openings, or hidden doors. I dropped onto the ground next to Rikki, and we sat in silence, turning off the lights to conserve the batteries.

After a few minutes, she spoke through the blackness. "I'm sorry, Chase."

"It wasn't your fault," I assured her.

"You could still be camping out on the beach if I hadn't brought all this trouble into your life."

My hand reached over in the dark and found her face. I pulled her close and kissed her.

When I broke off the kiss, I told her, "We're going to get out of here."

"What do you have in mind?"

"I guess I'm going to swim for it."

19

"I should go," Rikki insisted. "It's my fault we are stuck here."

"Rikki, I told you that this wasn't your doing. While I appreciate the concern, this is going to be dangerous. I don't have the slightest doubts in your abilities, but I've had some training."

She folded her arms in frustration.

"Look," I conceded, "odds are you'll get your chance. I'll probably drown, and you'll be forced to try yourself."

She let out a gasp of exasperation. "What if you try to be optimistic?"

With a smile, I assured her, "Fine. By tomorrow, we are going to be sipping champagne, naked on the deck of *Talitha*. You'll be so in awe of my incredulous rescue that you won't be able to keep your hands off me."

She joked, "You might die from that."

"I'd die happy," I retorted.

I gathered the 200 feet of rope into a coil next to the pool. Before I attempted to swim out, I had to find the exit. Once it was located, I was going to do a lot of reconnaissance before trying to make the final swim. I didn't care for the term "final swim," but once my brain latched onto it, I continued to come back to it.

"Drive me a piton here," I told Rikki.

With only three spikes left, I wanted to stretch them out. This one would serve as the base point. Once I found the opening, a second piton would have to be anchored underwater. That was going to be an arduous task. However, in the long run, it should shave some time off my swim.

Since the most significant obstacle I was going to face was the amount of time I would have to hold my breath, the rope would speed my descent and, with any luck, my passage through the tunnel. If the tunnel was even there. The cable would also serve as a guide back if I got into any trouble.

"Give me the light."

I stripped off my shirt and shorts to reduce any drag. Rikki gave me the belt she wore during her rappel down the shaft. The two remaining pitons and the hammer were attached with carabiner clips.

I'd give up just about anything for the pair of fins I left on the beach. While I love the water and everything about it, swimming has never been my strong suit. During some Corps training, I always fell into the middle to lower half of the pack as far as speed went. I've held my breath for two minutes many times without breaking a sweat. My record was three and a half, but I thought I was dead after. The issue was the distance I had to swim in those few minutes.

"You're secure," Rikki confirmed after tying the end of the rope to the piton. The other end was looped around my arm.

"Be right back," I promised her.

The water was icy. Colder than normal. No sun to warm the surface, I supposed as I kicked my way across the pool.

With three or four big gulps of air, I tried to fully oxygenate my blood before I submerged. As I followed the wall down, I searched the dark waters with the light.

A mental timer ticked off the seconds. I didn't want to exhaust myself during the initial search, and after 90 seconds, I surfaced.

"Chase?" Rikki called through the dark.

"I'm good!" I shouted back.

"Anything?"

"Not yet."

I dove under again and repeated the search. My hands worked my way down the wall, and I estimated I was thirty feet down from the pressure on my ears. The pool continued deeper still. The water diffused the beam of the light, and the bottom was still not visible.

Another 90 seconds ticked off the timer. I kicked toward the surface, worried that the entrance might have been covered up, either intentionally like the shaft or naturally from the passage of time.

After six dives, I still hadn't made it to the bottom. The only basis I was using was the time and pressure. Since moving aboard *Carina*, one of my favorite pastimes has been snorkeling or scuba diving. The changes in water pressure are consistent, and I'm very familiar with how the changes affect me, at least as deep as 80 feet. Most of my time is spent between 20 and 40 feet of water.

A minute and a half passed. I kicked my feet down. The light caught a shadow about 15 feet ahead. The timer in my head passed two minutes.

My fingers grabbed the wall, and I pulled myself down. The light illuminated an opening. I wanted to be sure this was the entrance before using the piton.

My lungs burned. The timer in my head told me I'd been down for two minutes and 15 seconds. With several strokes down, I found the bottom of the entrance, about 20 feet from the top.

Two minutes and 45 seconds. My lungs were aching now, begging for air. No time to drive a piton, so I kicked and pushed myself toward the surface.

At two minutes and 56 seconds, my head cleared the water, and I gasped for air.

"Chase?" Rikki called.

"I'm good," I repeated between deep heaves of breath.

The fingers on my right hand found a hold on the edge of the wall. My hand clung to the side as I steadied my breath. Almost three minutes under and I was begging for air. Would that be enough time to clear the tunnel, if the tunnel was even completely accessible? I wasn't sure.

My brain worked the problem, asking questions. How long was a submarine? Most of the ones I was familiar with were 50 to 60 feet, but a German sub, built almost a century ago, might have been smaller. The answers didn't help me either. The tunnel could have been 20 feet long or 100 feet long; it was a crap shoot.

Once I caught my breath, I decided it was time to anchor the next piton. Now that I knew where the entrance was, I saved a few seconds, and by the time my counter hit 42 seconds, I was just inside the entry. As I swam into it deeper, I sank to the floor.

One minute and seven seconds. The light rested on the bottom between my knees as I removed the piton and hammer. In normal circumstances, driving one of these spikes into rock is usually quick, but there's no momentum underwater.

No point in pulling the hammer too far back, so I kept the motions short and put as much force as possible into each strike. The metal pinged, and the hits became rhythmic. Ting. Ting. Ting.

Two minutes and ten seconds. The spike was about half an inch into the rock. I needed another inch to ensure it was secure. My wrist twisted in an attempt to increase the force of the blow.

Two minutes and 32 seconds. I tugged hard on the piton. No movement. Another pull.

Two minutes and 43 seconds. My lungs burned again. The end of the rope snaked into the eye of the piton, and I tied it tight. My head was swirling. Three minutes clicked past, and I began ascending the rope, hand over hand. My climb slowed, and my body begged for oxygen. I lost count of the seconds. I swallowed water as I tried to gasp for air. Once I broke the surface, I started spewing salt water.

Rikki's hands grabbed me by my hair, the only thing she was able to reach. My right hand reached up for her arm, and she dragged me to the edge.

"Are you okay?" she asked as I vomited up the sea water.

Nodding, I coughed and sputtered. After spitting out more water, I caught my breath and heaved myself up on the edge.

Rikki dug in her pack and pulled out a bottle of water. I took a couple of slow sips as I sat on the edge of the pool.

"I found the entrance," I muttered. "One piton down."

"How much line do you have?" she asked.

"I don't know," I admitted, "but not enough."

After handing her the bottle back, I lay back on the stone floor.

"Think you can do it?" she asked, her voice trembling.

"Once I anchor the next piton, I should be able to cover the first 200 feet fast. Less than a minute, maybe 45 seconds. We just have to hope that there are not a few hundred yards of tunnel after that."

"You need to rest," she urged me. It was futile. I wasn't moving for a few minutes anyway.

A few minutes turned into a bit more as I drifted to sleep. In the back of my mind, I heard Rikki moving about. When I woke up, the cave was dark.

"Rikki?" I called out.

"I'm here," she answered, clicking the light on.

She was lying near the water. As I sat up, she looked at me. "You've been sleeping a bit."

"How long?"

"An hour."

The groggy aura that lingers after a power nap hung on me. If I dropped my head back, I would doze off again. Instead, I fought the urge and sat up.

"I have to anchor the last piton," I said loudly.

"Grab a bite to eat," Rikki urged. She offered me one of the protein bars we packed early this morning. It seemed like that had been days ago.

I snatched the chocolate chip and coconut bar and devoured it in three bites. It was getting late in the afternoon. The clock on Rikki's camera indicated it was almost four in the afternoon. Just under three hours till sunset.

With my flashlight hooked to my belt, along with the last piton and hammer, I dropped into the water. By using the rope, I pulled myself under quickly. Twenty seconds ticked by when I reached the first piton.

I grabbed the rest of the rope and swam hard into the tunnel. When the line paid out, I sank to the bottom and started planting the last spike.

My timer told me a minute and seven seconds. The steel spike seemed to set faster. My technique was improving, and if I had one more, I bet my time would cut in half.

One minute and 52 seconds. The spike was anchored, and despite some effort to pull it free, it wasn't going anywhere.

Hand over hand, I ascended the rope until my head broke the surface at two minutes and 41 seconds. My chest ached, but there wasn't an oxygen deficit.

"Done," I told her as I pulled myself out of the water.

"How are you?" she knelt beside me.

"I'm good. I covered a lot of ground that time."

She handed me the bottle of water. After taking a sip, I explained, "The rope makes a big difference."

Rikki sat beside me and stuck her feet in the water. "Are you sure about this?"

I sighed, "Unless you can sprout wings, I don't see another way."

She sighed. Her body trembled in the dark.

I inhaled a deep breath and told her, "It is going to take me a while to get back here."

"How long do I wait?"

"Give me till tomorrow. You have enough protein bars to last you a day or two. Conserve your water. You might find some dripping off a wall too. Save that for a last resort."

"Chase..."

"Look," I tried to reassure her by wrapping my arm around her shoulder, "I don't know if you realize this about me, but I'm a tough son of a bitch. This is just a little swim."

"Oh, I realize how tough you are." Her voice lifted, and I heard the smile in her tone.

My arms wrapped around her as I kissed her in the dark.

"Now?" she asked as I stood up.

"It's getting late. I would like to have some daylight left once I get clear of the cave."

"Please be careful," she urged. "I don't want you to forget me down here."

"Don't worry," I promised, "the last thing I'll do is forget about you."

I stripped off the belt that held the hammer and flashlight, reducing as much weight as possible. Leaving the flashlight meant I would swim in the dark, but my hands would be free and hopefully speed me along.

I spent the next minute inhaling and exhaling in an attempt to fill my blood with the most oxygen. Then, with one last gulp, I dove into the pool. The thought that went through my head was, "I hope that's not my last breath."

I started the timer in my head as soon as I hit the water. My hands caught the line and began churning fist over fist along the rope. My eyes were open, but all I saw was black.

When I reached the first piton, my fingers scraped across the steel, and I leveled off in the tunnel. The second spike was the point of no return.

I'd moved fast so far. Just under a minute at 56 seconds. When I released the rope, my feet kicked with furious fervor. My fingers stretching out and grabbing for anything to propel me forward. The tunnel was nothing but an abyss, and my heart was pounding in my ears.

I released a blast of carbon dioxide. Not enough to empty my lungs, just as some weird comfort. As if the release was telling my body to just hang on. There will be some air soon.

The two minute mark rolled past, and I was still kicking forward.

Two minutes and thirty seconds. I'd long passed the time when a return trip was safe. After that, there was no going back.

My lungs were burning. Some strange thought crossed my mind. I hadn't talked to my sister in weeks–more like months.

No time for that, Chase.

My feet pedaled harder. Two minutes and 45 seconds. My chest squeezed, and I let out another quick burst of air.

Three minutes.

Come on, Chase.

My fingertips scratched the bottom, and I knew I was slowing some.

Three minutes and ten seconds. Longer than I had been down setting the pitons. Still not my record, but closer than I ever wanted to get.

The blackness ahead seemed to change–a purplish blob instead of a dark mass.

Three minutes and 15 seconds.

Light. I saw light. My body wanted to give up, take a breath of water, and just rest.

Keep going. There was a reason to stop.

My fingers caught the edge of an opening, and I saw the sea open up in front of me. I pushed off the bottom as I tried to kick toward the surface.

The edges of my vision closed in. There was darkness creeping back.

I thought I was out of the tunnel. My feet tried to move, and I let out the last of the carbon dioxide in my lungs.

I had to inhale.

No, I tried to tell myself.

My body demanded it. My feet were slowing, and everything tilted.

And darkness entangled me.

20

Waves thrashed my body against the rock as I coughed sea water from my lungs. As the water receded, it gathered momentum to pummel me again. My fingertips caught on the edge of the boulder jutting up from the sea. My arms pulled my weight up. Finally, I found a moment of respite where I could catch my breath.

I didn't know how I made it to the surface. Was I almost there when I passed out?

Red streaks tinged the surface, and my hand found the gash on my shoulder. The jagged rock must have sliced through my skin.

As I clung to the top of the boulder, I attempted to catch my breath. My throat and lungs were burning from the salt water. My stomach convulsed, and I vomited into the surf. After several seconds, I was dry-heaving.

I tried to get my bearings as I splashed the salt water on my face. I was on the northwestern side of the island. The sun was in the middle of the western sky; two hours, at most, until dark. I had to get off this rock and make it back to *Talitha*.

My right foot found a hold, and I pushed up higher on the rock. The waves were coming in fast, and I struggled as they threw me into the rock. The safest way to avoid being beaten against the stone any more was to jump out as the surf pulled back. I'd be fighting the surf the whole time, but I should be able to stay clear of the rocks.

As the water pulled back, I could make out other rocks and boulders just under the surface. Once I made the dive, I needed to swim away from the cliffs, at least 50 feet. That would keep me clear of this meat grinder.

When the next wave crashed up against the rock, I launched myself over it. As my body rose, I caught a breath before diving under the next wave.

After I surfaced again, I began stroking away from the island. After twenty seconds, I angled north and began swimming, keeping the island just off my right shoulder.

By my best guess, we anchored *Talitha* three miles away. Even under normal conditions, I'd be a steady but slow swimmer. After the free dive out of the cavern and the thrashing the rocks gave me, I was making slow time.

Rikki lingered in my mind. She had no way of knowing if I made it out or not. That type of purgatory might wear on her. At some point, she'd assume I wasn't coming for her, and she'd attempt to make the same swim.

I rolled onto my back to rest for a few seconds. Whoever dropped the grenades down the shaft had no doubt seen *Talitha* anchored off shore. The tactical thing would be to disable the vessel.

After what my arms were sure was an eternity, I rounded the island. A wave of relief came over me as I laid eyes on the yacht, still floating. The sun was dropping into the traditional tropical sunset. Had I not been in the water for several hours now, I might have found myself on deck with a cold beer and my feet propped toward the western sky.

Talitha lay at anchor 300 yards from me. Images of food crossed my mind. The protein bar earlier had sustained me, but now that I saw the end of this journey, I stroked steadily toward the ship.

My head came up for a second, and I wanted to keep my bearings. Something caught my attention. The tender that we had taken ashore was tied up to the stern of the yacht.

Treading water, I watched the boat for a minute. A figure moved across the aft deck. The man on deck stared past me at the sunset. He took a cigarette out and lighted it as he enjoyed the view. He seemed oblivious to me, and I tried to sink down enough to remain hidden, keeping my feet and hands rotating underwater to hold me in place.

After the sun disappeared, the sky turned a deep purple, and the stars glistened overhead. Finally, it was dark enough that he wouldn't be able to make out my movement, and I began swimming again toward the boat.

He had taken a different tactic. Make sure that if we somehow escaped being buried, he would be there when we came back to the boat. Only he was lazy. The hours passed and nothing happened, so he relaxed. He probably found my tuna sandwiches. He started to enjoy himself, even coming into the open to watch the sunset.

Sloppy work. It would cost him. I was pissed, and three hours in the water trying to escape only to find one of my would-be murderers waiting on my oasis. It infuriated me more.

By the time I reached *Talitha*, the sun had moved on to other parts of the Earth, and the ocean was dark. My progress slowed as I switched from stroking over-hand to a silent approach. The choice to make the approach underwater was nixed by my brain. I'd spent enough time underwater for today. My chances were better on the surface.

I skirted the boat and approached the bow. The anchor chain stretched out from the windlass on the pulpit. My hands wrapped around the half-inch stainless-steel chain, I pulled myself up out of the water. The pulpit was close to 20 feet above the waterline. My damp hands slipped as I attempted to climb. After getting another grip, I continued ascending. I didn't want to cause the boat to make any quick movements, but the worry was futile. The Nomad was much heavier than my sailboat, and the motions I was making weren't enough to cause more than a slight bounce. Something easily attributed to the waves.

My arms stretched upward to grab the pulpit, and I hoisted myself over the rail. While standing on the foredeck in a pair of boxers, I didn't feel like a threat.

I crouched as I moved aft. The first thing I needed to do was establish how many men were aboard.

While staying on the port side, I peered through the windows. The upper lounge deck was clear. The lights were all on. It was careless, like being on deck; they were announcing their presence.

Like the men on Big Pine, they, or he, were simply following orders.

"Make sure they don't come back to the boat" or something like that. He didn't think we would make it back, so he's enjoying himself.

As I stepped into the lounge, I listened for movement. There was no talking. Maybe it was just the one guy. With a peek down the stairs, I didn't see anyone. The balls of my feet touched lightly on each step.

A blond man reclined on the same couch where the detective had left me and where Rikki and I first skipped a meal in lieu of other activities. His back was toward me; he appeared to be resting if not sleeping, judging by the slow rhythmic up and down of his shoulders.

Despite straining my ears, I couldn't make out anyone else on board. Not wanting to waste this man's vulnerability, I stepped off the stairs and wrapped my arm around his throat. There were some questions I wanted to ask him, and his remaining alive would be pertinent to getting those answers.

"Ach!" he grunted as my forearm cut off his air. His right arm reached for his waist, where a pearl handled .45 was hooked under his waistband. My left hand swept toward the gun, swatting his hand away.

"What the hell!" someone shouted behind me.

Cursing, I rolled over the couch, still gripping the blond's neck. Sometime mid-roll, I decided his answers didn't matter. My forearm tightened and twisted until the audible crack echoed through the room.

The voice behind me belonged to a six-foot brute that charged me when he heard the blond's neck snap. My left hand came back from the blond's waist with the pearl-handled grip in my palm. The first shot hit Hulk in his thigh, taking him down to his knees.

Shock washed over his face, and his right hand fumbled toward his back. He was going for a gun, I assumed, as I squeezed a second shot into his chest. He fell onto his back, sprawled with his left foot hooked on his right calf.

I held my position and waited for the commotion to draw anyone else out. A full minute passed, and the boat was silent. After standing up, I made a quick circuit of the vessel, ensuring that I was the only one on board.

Apparently, these guys came in pairs. Blondie and the Brute sported similar tattoos to the men trying to kidnap Rikki. Once I dragged both of the bodies out of the lounge, I started cleaning any blood. The big one's leg wound caused the most trouble, leaving a small pool of brown on the carpet. After a quick scrubbing, the stain seemed to vanish. My sanitation efforts wouldn't hold up against an ultraviolet light, but to the untrained eye, there didn't seem to be anything amiss.

After covering the bodies with the canvas dinghy cover, I found my way to the kitchen and made up a peanut butter sandwich. Timing was going to be an issue. I needed to dispose of the two goons, and I knew exactly where to do it.

I made up two more sandwiches and wrapped them up. After hoisting both bodies over the rail, I let them drop to the swim platform, where I could load them into the dinghy.

I slipped into a pair of shorts and some sandals that might have belonged to Sam and cut the lights off, leaving only the anchor light illuminated. I retrieved a 200-foot spool of dock line, from one of the stern lockers, along with two more flashlights.

It took a while to navigate the shoreline in the dark. Prudence required me to keep the outboard at idle speed. Enough momentum to move me forward but slow enough that I could watch for hazards.

The rocky beach where we anchored early this morning was still empty. So as soon as I cut the engine, I pulled up the motor and jumped into the water to drag the inflatable boat ashore.

After wrapping the spool of line across my neck and shoulder, I pulled the corpse of the big guy up so that I could get my shoulder under the center of his mass and lift him up. There wasn't much I could do except make two trips.

A wheelbarrow would have been handy, but Rikki didn't keep one on *Talitha*. Once I made the initial climb over the rocky embankment, the rest of the trip would be a slow slope. So I readjusted the hulk once I got past the rocks, pointed myself toward the house, and trudged through the scrub.

With the added weight and my body's growing exhaustion, the hike took close to an hour. During my trek, I worried about getting Rikki out. However, the dock line would suffice for climbing rope, and I should have no trouble hoisting her up.

My thoughts turned over how these two had found us. They weren't alone; someone dropped them off. Everything told me Richman was involved, but there was something about his demeanor that made me think he wasn't in charge. He was too weaselly. Those types of people don't garner followers. They might get promoted in the military, but their subordinates have a hard time with their command.

No, Richman was a player, but he wasn't the lead dog. There was something more organized about this. Every time it had been a two-man team. Men that were brought in to kill and hurt. They might have had some ideals, whether or not they were screwed up, but these men did nothing out of a selfless desire to further their cause.

As I reached the top of the island, the moon had risen, the crescent smile reflected off the water below. The brute's weight dropped off my shoulder, releasing the tension. He thudded onto the ground. My lights found the piton that Rikki had anchored at the top, still embedded in the rock. The boys with the grenades hadn't dislodged it. The same might not be said for the ones along the walls of the shaft. I had no intention of relying on them, anyway.

The knot from the first rope was still bound to the piton. Two feet of rope dangled into the shaft. After stripping it off, I threaded the line through the eye of the piton. As I stretched some slack in the line from the piton, I wrapped the rope around the waist of the dead man, giving me close to ten feet of line hanging between him and the spike. The other end dropped down the shaft.

I knelt down, shouting down the hole. "Rikki!"

A muffled reply echoed back.

"Repeat that!"

The sea breeze created enough noise that her voice was being drowned out.

"I can't understand you," I hollered. "Tug the rope twice."

The line jerked twice.

"Great, tie the line around you. When you are ready to start up, give me three sharp tugs."

The line pulled twice.

While I waited for her to get ready, I found a sturdy footing, so that my feet would have something to push against as I brought her up. A few feet of line gathered from below the piton as I got ready to heave.

When the three sharp tugs came, I gave her a warning shout before I started hoisting her up. Despite Rikki's diminutive size, she was still dead weight. Until she got inside the shaft, she couldn't do anything to assist.

As soon as she reached the wall of the shaft, I felt her do something. Likely using her feet to "walk" up the wall. The progress was slow, relying on me to keep a solid grip with one hand as I switched to the next.

My arms were tired, but the sound of her scraping her feet against the shaft echoed.

The rope snapped, and a scream echoed out of the ground. The line singed my palm as it sliced through my hand. I twisted my hand to slow the rope over my wrist, and the sudden jolt jerked me forward.

"Chase!" Rikki howled from below.

My left foot caught a rock on the edge of the hole. I would not be able to hold my position long enough to get another grip. The rock jiggled under my foot. When it snapped, I skidded over the edge. My hand caught the piton, and I flipped the slack I had gathered over the spike before I lost my grip.

We were dangling by one piton rated for a couple hundred pounds. My hands gripped the line hanging over either side of the piton.

"Rikki?" I hollered.

"I'm here."

"Watch out," I shouted as I released the line holding her.

My weight pulled her toward the surface as I fell. She rose past me as I dropped. The line I was holding jerked as the rope around the corpse tightened, pulling the body toward the ledge.

Rikki screamed as the brute tumbled over the edge. He fell about ten feet before the rope, wrapped around the piton, snapped tight. The three of us hung in the hole.

"I got it!" Rikki exclaimed.

My hand burned as I glanced up to see her reaching for the edge. Once she got to the edge, the weight would shift again, and I wasn't sure what would happen. Right now, the corpse outweighed me enough to counterbalance.

The tension slacked for a second before shifting again. I rose a foot; something was holding me and the hulk up. A shift could send us both to the bottom of the cave, a fall I didn't think would fare well with me.

"Can you tie off the rope?" I shouted up as I scanned the wall for a hand hold. I finally saw one if I could get closer without falling.

"Got it!"

Gently, I swayed toward the wall and reached for the jutting rock. My fingertips caught the lip and pulled me closer. Finally, my foot hooked on another lip, and I rested.

"What do I do?" Rikki shouted.

"I can't see to climb out," I answered. "Can you pull him up without dropping him?"

"I guess," she uttered. Her tone was cautious.

Turning skyward, I could see I was only 25 or so feet from the top. The body hung about ten feet down.

Rikki grunted as she pulled the body up. After several minutes, she gasped in relief.

"Are you okay?" she called.

"For now," I confirmed.

"What now?"

After testing my grip, I responded, "I've got my own weight. He has about 70 pounds on me. You just have to make sure the piton is clear so we can use it as a pulley."

"Why don't I pull you up?" she suggested.

"This should work."

"Chase!" she snapped. "Tie that damned rope around you. I'm pulling you up."

"I can't tie anything," I told her.

"Ugh," she cried. "Hold on please."

With only my right arm, I wrapped the rope around my elbow and forearm. My hand gripped it. Blood was oozing out of my fist.

"Tell me when you're ready," I ordered her.

"I guess."

"I'm letting go in three... two... one." My feet jumped off the wall. I felt gravity take hold as I started down for a millisecond before I started going up. The corpse lowered past me, slowed by my weight.

"My hand," Rikki announced, and I reached for her extended arm.

She pulled me over the edge, and I released the rope. The weight of the corpse, no longer hindered by me, dropped. The dock line whirred as it zipped around the piton until the end fluttered down the hole.

I let out an exhausted curse as Rikki wrapped her arms around me.

"My bag," I muttered.

"What?" she pulled away.

"There's a peanut butter sandwich in there for you."

21

Where we anchored didn't seem safe. So, after carrying Blondie up the hill and dropping him with his friend, we made our way back to *Talitha*.

"We have to move her," I explained. "I don't want to wake up in the middle of the night being boarded by more of the Third Reich."

"Where are we going to go?"

The next island was 30 miles south. In the daylight, *Talitha* would be able to cover it in a couple of hours. At night, I'd take it slow. We might find a place to drop anchor close to dawn.

Rikki offered to drive, figuring that she had longer to rest while I made my swim for freedom. After agreeing with her, I curled up on the bench on the bridge and dropped off to sleep before she suggested my going below.

When I opened my eyes, I heard a pinging sound.

"What's that?"

"The radar. There's a boat out there?"

After sitting up, I looked at the screen. The radar was picking up something two miles to the east.

"Does the AIS say anything?"

The automatic identification system works with the radar. It can identify a vessel by name if that vessel has the system, and the captain has it turned on.

"No," she acknowledged.

She wore a worried look.

"That doesn't mean anything," I assured her. "I know lots of pleasure boats that don't even have radar."

She stared out the bridge window into the night. The radar continued to ding. The boat was making a slow progression.

"How long have I been asleep?"

"Couple of hours," she informed me.

"Your turn," I urged her as I wrapped my arms around her.

Her hand slipped off the helm and rested on mine. She twisted her head so that her lips lined up with mine.

After a second, she pulled away, saying, "I'm fine."

Her eyes cut to the radar again.

"What if they were supposed to make contact?" she asked.

"Nothing we can do about that," I told her. "I thought about asking some questions, but we never got around to it."

"Should I call Oder in the morning?" she asked me.

"I don't think it was him," I shared.

"Why do you say that?"

"It occurred to me that he knew where we were going."

She nodded.

"But," I added, "it's possible Richman knew about Baxter's submarine base. Or they are tracking us."

"How?"

"Richman had an airplane. Between a small boat and an aircraft, they could have kept eyes on us all the way from Bimini without us noticing."

"I didn't see anyone when we were at the castle," she pointed out. "We had a clear view of the entire horizon."

"A plane can come out of nowhere in just a few minutes."

"I guess," she conceded.

"And a tiny boat can blend in pretty well. When I was coming up on the boat, the blond guy stared at me while he smoked an entire cigarette and never realized I was watching him. Like missing the trees for the forest."

"I think you have that backwards."

I offered a nonchalant shrug.

"But Oder?"

"Call it instinct," I explained. "He dropped the name of a friend of mine. If they know each other, I doubt he has nefarious intentions."

She smiled at me. "Those are some big words there, Marine."

"I like to read the dictionary."

"I don't think we gained much from our visit though."

"We got to tour a submarine base," I told her.

"And almost died there," she countered. "Several times."

"But we didn't."

"I'm wondering," she pondered, "why did they try to kill us? The other day they seemed to want to kidnap me, but now they've changed tactics."

"Perhaps we've become too big of a threat. Maybe they didn't like that we found our way to Darby Island."

She glanced at the radar again.

"Are they following us?" she asked.

"They are keeping their distance," I noted. "Want me to take the dinghy and go check them out?"

She shook her head. "It's almost dawn. I have a better idea."

She motioned for me to take the helm before she climbed down the steps and vanished from the bridge. Despite the couple of hours of sleep, I was still groggy. When Rikki made it back, I would go down and start a pot of coffee.

The eastern sky was showing the first shades of light. Nothing more than the tinge of purple creeping over the horizon. Sunrise in the Bahamas was as impressive as the sunsets, but most people didn't bother with it. It was even possible to spot the green flash at sunrise, but most people slept through it. Not that I was any less guilty. I enjoyed far more sunsets than I did sunrises.

Rikki reappeared on the steps.

"What if we fly over and check them out," she suggested, showing me the case she carried.

When she unlatched it, she revealed a high-dollar drone.

"Where do you get all these wonderful toys?"

"Didn't I tell you?" she asked and answered, "My daddy's rich."

"What's the range?"

"It'll go up to five miles before it loses the radio signal. Once it does, it switches to autopilot and returns to the remote."

She removed a remote that sported three joystick controls, several buttons, and a small screen.

"We can see everything it does, as long as it is in transmission range. If not, the video saves on an SD card."

As I marveled at the device, I asked, "Does it have IR?"

"Night-vision?" she asked. "No, it only records black when it's dark."

"It should be light soon," I pointed out. "Let's stay on course. As long as they stay about two miles out, we shouldn't have an issue. Until the sun comes up though, I want to maintain a watch on deck. It would be easy to slip a small dinghy under the radar."

She nodded.

"You take the helm," I told her. "I'll be on the aft deck. That'll be the most likely point they'd try to board while we are moving."

When I relinquished the helm, I left the pearl-handled .45 I took off Blondie resting on the control panel. The brute's weapon, a cheap 9 mm, was stashed under the cushion in the lounge. It would work for me.

Talitha's wake glowed in the waning moonlight. While pacing along the deck overlooking the swim platform, I had 180 degrees sightline around the stern of the yacht. There was little chance that any of the guys we had come up against had the skill to attempt boarding a moving vessel at the bow. Not an impossibility, but I regarded it as unlikely.

The engines beneath my feet droned on. The din felt like it was in my body. Another reminder of what I love about sailing. The silence, or rather, the natural sounds. The sound of the hull slicing through the water. Waves crashing as I bounce through them, the birds that take refuge on my spreaders before continuing on their journey. All those sounds are lost in the mechanical hum of the diesel engines.

The sun was peeking over the horizon–a tiny orange curve on a vast blue canvas. A clear sky allowed the orange-yellow glow of the sunrise to spread. A small arc became a sphere as it climbed over the surface of the sea.

From our viewpoint on the bridge, the ocean was clear. A small dot toward the west was the boat in question. They seemed to be moving about the same speed and direction as we were.

With the coast clear for a few minutes, I returned to the flybridge. Rikki had set up the drone and was waiting for me to launch it.

"Do we need to stop the engines?" I asked.

"Shouldn't matter, but let's cut them down to idle."

We were in 37 feet of water and miles from shore. We were safe to drift for a few minutes. Rikki stood back as the drone's propellers lifted it off the deck.

The aircraft moved off the stern of the vessel at Rikki's command. The screen showed the ocean as the drone soared higher. When it was a few hundred feet off the ocean's surface, she directed the drone toward the target.

The video was high-definition, and as she zoomed the lens, I distinguished the drops of water flying off each wave. Finally, the boat came into view.

She was a trawler-type power boat about 45 feet long. I wasn't familiar with the make, but she was an older model. She was built sometime in the 80s, but she looked well maintained. The wooden rails were recently varnished, and the hull paint looked fresh. Blue letters on the transom spelled "*Miss Erica.*"

"Can they see the drone?" I asked.

"If they look up," she told me, "but it's quiet, and most people don't notice it."

I peered over her shoulder to watch the screen. The deck of *Miss Erica* was clear. A figure stood on the bridge, but the sun's reflection off the glass made distinguishing anything about the person impossible.

"They're moving about eight to ten knots," I commented. "Not in much of a rush."

"Do you think they're following us?" Rikki questioned.

"I don't think so. Let's keep an eye on it for a minute."

The boat churned through the waves as the drone followed along a few hundred feet behind them. Rikki adjusted the altitude as the ship continued southeast, allowing the aircraft to rise.

A figure came out on the aft deck.

"That looks like a woman," I observed.

Rikki adjusted the camera when another person appeared. Both were older, their white hair reflecting in the sun.

"Are they... naked?" I asked.

"Uh..." she stammered as she pulled the camera back.

The two people embraced in a passionate kiss as a third appeared.

"Okay," I confessed, "I've seen enough."

"Shit," she mumbled, and I glanced back at the screen. The three people were all nude and pointing toward the camera. "They spotted the drone."

"Time to make a retreat," I insisted.

"Oh," she uttered, and curiosity drew my attention back to the screen where two women and a man were waving body parts at us while laughing hysterically.

Rikki snorted in laughter as she steered the drone away from the vessel.

"Great," I joked, "we're voyeurs."

The chuckling from Rikki turned into a bellowing howl as she laughed. I was laughing with her, and when the radio chirped, we were both startled.

A female voice came over the speaker. "Unknown vessel, this is the *Motor Vessel, Miss Erica*. We hope you enjoyed the show."

Rikki grabbed the microphone on the VHF radio. "*Miss Erica*, we apologize for the intrusion. We were playing with a new toy. We are sorry."

The woman responded, "Don't be sorry, sweetie. The best part of the show was still to come. If you know what I mean."

Rikki tried to control her giggle as she responded, "Affirmative."

"If you're going our way," the woman offered, "drinks will be on us."

"Thank you," was all Rikki was able to utter.

The radio went silent. We stared at each other in a mixture of mirth and embarrassment.

"Guess we're having drinks with them?"

"Hell, no," she retorted. "You want someone naked, you're stuck with me."

Pulling her close, I kissed her. "I'm good with that."

She stepped back and slipped the tank top she was wearing over her head. "I hope we don't drift too far," she teased.

22

The bed was empty when I woke up. After rolling to my side, I let my feet drop to the floor. The hatches were open, and the cabin had a steady breeze carrying the salt air into the room. My clothes were nowhere to be found, and the thought occurred to me that Rikki was having some fun with me after our encounter with *Miss Erica* this morning. She misjudged me if she thought I wouldn't venture on deck unclothed.

We dropped anchor by eight o'clock just off a small is-land. Mushu Cay if I recall correctly. We ate breakfast in the nude before heading back to bed where we attempted another bout. Instead, we ended up asleep in each other's arms.

My feet padded into the corridor. Rikki's voice was coming from below, and I paused. Who was she talking to? I couldn't make out what she was saying, but her tone wasn't distressed.

As I followed her voice, I descended the spiral stairwell from the upper deck. Rikki was standing in the galley with a phone to her ear. She was also naked, taking a cue from *Miss Erica*.

"Thank you, Milo," she spoke into the phone. "I'll get it now."

I found some juice in the refrigerator and poured myself a glass. Rikki laid the phone on the counter and turned toward me.

"Where're my clothes?" I asked her.

"Is that all you can think about?"

With a smile, I answered, "Not at all. Just trying to get my bearings in case anyone shows up."

Her hand touched my chest, and she whispered, "I think we have some unfinished business from earlier."

"Oh yeah. Why don't you tell me what Milo had to say?"

"He reached out to an acquaintance in the records department...I guess for the C.I.A. His friend found Rusty Adams's report after the fact. He's going to email me the file."

"Did he say what it said?"

"The basics. He stowed aboard the submarine when it left Darby Island. He sabotaged one of the torpedoes. It exploded eight hours after they left Darby Island."

"Was it submerged?" I asked.

"Seems to have been. Adams escaped through an airlock. He had to swim to the surface. From there he swam north for 30 hours where he came ashore on an island. A fisherman rescued him six weeks later."

"Damn, he was a bad ass."

Rikki laughed.

I added matter-of-factly, "Milo said he was a Marine."

"I guess an Army man couldn't do that?" she asked in jest.

"He could, but he'd whine about it after."

She rolled her eyes at me. "Machismo isn't always sexy, you know?"

With a shrug, I asked, "Did he say which island?"

"I don't know," she remarked. "I'm waiting on the email."

"Well, what do you want to do while we wait?"

Her arms twisted around my neck, and she launched herself up, wrapping her legs around me. I kissed her and carried her to the couch.

When we rolled onto the floor, she stared down at me. Her brown eyes were wide with an awe and anticipation in life. It wasn't a look I'd only seen during sex. She had a tendency to view everything that way. She was excited to be wherever she was.

Most people don't grasp that freedom. They can't enjoy the now. Rikki might have been able to do that because her financial situation allowed her few worries. She could have been one of those "ladies who lunch" and carried about in high society, or at least Hollywood elite society. But I didn't think so.

Instead, she wanted to gallivant around the Caribbean, looking for treasure. She didn't just seek adventure. This woman imbued it. I had a feeling that I would want to look up in her eyes forever, and she would find the monotony of that abhorrent. Eventually.

For the moment, she kissed me, and I kissed her back.

As we lay on our backs, we stared at the ceiling. The designer of this boat saw fit to create a textured ceiling, something I didn't understand, unless he enjoyed cleaning ridges.

"Might want to check your email," I suggested.

She rolled over and smiled at me. "Tired?"

"Rikki, dear, I swam like 400 miles yesterday and that was nothing compared to your endurance."

"We should get you on some vitamins."

I sat up, pushing her back. "Check your email. I have an idea."

"Where are you going?"

"Bridge. Come up when you have the email."

On the bridge, I pulled out the paper charts. Technology has almost rendered the old-fashioned paper versions useless, or so the electronics and software companies want you to believe. To some extent, the paper charts were outdated. The ones in the navigation table I pulled out were printed nearly ten years ago. Obstructions, shoals, and even islands have changed over the last decade. The electronic versions are updated far more often, and some are even user-updated, allowing for recent changes to be marked as cruisers come across them.

For this search, nothing beats a physical map. Sure, computers can do all the triangulation, but I'm not the computer-savvy guy that can plug in the data.

What I can do, though, is take three reference points and narrow down the area with a ruler and a pencil. Darby Island was the first point in question. The submarine we were searching for left the hidden base. Cuba was its likely destination.

With a clear ruler from the desk, I traced a direct line from Darby Island to Cuba. If the submarine's ultimate destination was closer to Havana, it would need to make a course change approximately 100 to 130 miles from Baxter's Nazi hideaway. But, if the report that Adams filed was accurate, the boat never made it that far.

Submarines travel about as slow as sailboats. I wasn't sure what the average speed was, but I figured eight to ten knots per hour. If the submarine sank eight hours after leaving port, it would be somewhere between 60 and 80 miles from Darby Island.

I sighed as I stared at the chart. So if the submarine traveled much slower than eight knots per hour, she would have sunk somewhere in the Tongue of the Ocean. The Tongue is one of the few stretches of water in the Bahamas where the recorded depth is over 1000 feet deep. Some places reach over 4000 feet. If Adams sabotaged the U-boat there, it might have settled into a grave too deep for the two of us to find it, much less resurrect it.

Rikki's footsteps sounded on the steps. She carried her laptop with her.

"Get your email?"

"I did," she boasted, laying the computer on top of the charts and folding the screen open.

The screen showed a PDF copy of a hand-written log. The scrawled letters were familiar, matching the logbook that Oder shared with us.

Over the next few minutes, I read the entry, noting the details of time and distance.

"Adams said he found himself on a cay south of Andros Island," I noted, circling the bottom coastline of the sizeable Bahamian island.

"He stated he survived on the small island by fishing," Rikki pointed out. "That's insane."

Nodding, I agreed, "But we don't know which island."

"Wait," Rikki interjected, "I read something in here. There at the bottom"

After scrolling to the bottom of the scanned document, I stared at the screen. Rikki tapped her finger on the line.

"The fisherman that rescued him," she explained. "He told Adams that normally he fished the waters 20 miles north at High Point Cay."

I traced my finger along the coastline of Andros Island, looking for a High Point Cay.

"There's a High Point," I noted, "but it's not an island."

"Maybe it was an island back in those days," Rikki observed.

"We are making a lot of suppositions," I told her. "No evidence to back us up."

Rikki offered a nonchalant grin.

By measuring a radius of 20 miles south of High Point, I used the ruler to draw an arc that resembled a smile. Three small islands fell within a tolerable distance to the smile.

"How long did it take him to swim?"

Rikki answered, "He said 30 hours."

"He was lying," I suggested.

"He didn't swim it?" she wondered.

"No, he exaggerated," I explained. "What's the rule of thumb for exaggeration? Ten percent?"

Rikki laughed, "Judging from the guys I've been with, it might be higher."

I cut my eyes at her.

"Present company excluded, of course."

"Let's say he swam between 20 and 30 hours," I told her. "Given that time frame, we should say he covered an average of one mile per hour."

My ruler and pencil started to work again. Three more smiles formed equidistant from the three islands we marked. Once I drew a circle around the congruence, I stared at a search area of close to 2,000 square miles.

"Is that where you think it is?" Rikki asked.

"Roughly, yes," I answered, adding, "but everything east of here is pointless."

After marking the edge of the Tongue of the Ocean, I cut two-thirds of the circle off.

"That's still a sizable piece of ocean," I amended. "I don't have any idea how we can find it."

Rikki smiled, exposing the whites of her teeth. "I got something for that," she explained. "Follow me."

We descended all the way to the engine room. Rikki pulled open a storeroom hatch. On the floor sat a rectangular metal machine.

"A submersible?" I questioned.

"Yep," she beamed. "A Roving Underwater Metal Alloy Detective Vehicle. It's designed specifically to search for wreckage, cargo, or anything metal. It operates just like the drone, only it requires no control. Once we input the search pattern, this baby will scour the bottom of the ocean until it detects metal."

"How far can it go?" I asked.

"It can do a 70 square mile radius in 12 hours. After that it has to return to its base to recharge."

"I'm serious. Where did you get this?"

"Bought it," she boasted. "It's a $2 million investment."

My eyebrows lifted in shock.

"Cool, right?"

My head shook in disbelief. I had trouble swallowing a $2 million dollar underwater Roomba.

23

Six days. For six days we were anchored in 20 feet of crystal blue water. Pure, unadulterated paradise. Not one single soul had passed our way in the last week.

Since the rover could only search 70 square miles, I found a central spot to moor *Talitha*. From there, we could launch several search patterns without being forced to relocate. We programmed the coordinates into the computer, launched the rover, and waited. After 12 hours, the little robot would return to recharge its batteries overnight.

We repeated the process six times, and we were only forced to move the boat once to maximize the search area. So while we waited on the rover to do its sniffing around, we enjoyed being anchored out 20 miles from any land. The solar panels affixed to the top of *Talitha* and the diesel engines kept the batteries topped off and the lights working.

The open anchorage had no barriers above or below the surface, making it a rollier mooring than I would have preferred, and I was grateful that we weren't in *Carina*. My monohull would have been rocking in every direction with the wind and the waves. The broad-beamed yacht still rocked, but the effects were tolerable.

Luckily, Rikki's stock of toys included a spear pole, along with a mask, and fins. So I took some time after launching the rover every morning to snorkel and search out a fresh catch.

There wasn't much on the sea floor except sand. Scattered about the bottom, some small formations provided shelter for small fish, which brings in the bigger fish. On the first dive, I'd snagged two lionfish and a medium-sized lobster.

Today, I was just hovering on the surface, watching the area around a jagged rock covered with fan coral. My hunting ground today was about 30 yards off the bow of *Talitha*. The water lapped over my back. The water in the Bahamas is often quite chilly, and the warmth of the sun on my back, while the rest of my body was submerged in cold water, is an unusual but enjoyable sensation.

A ray soared over the sandy bottom. The tips of its wings flapped in slow, rhythmic motions to propel it along in what appeared to be a frivolous and lackadaisical direction.

Stingray can be delicious, but I had yet to prepare one. The ray was one of those creatures I never speared. For me, it was like hunting eagles. They were there to be admired. That was it. While there's no real rhyme or reason that I should have some aversion to eating a ray over a lionfish or snapper, I did. The same could be said about dogs and cows.

I floated over the ray as he swept over the sand, sucking up the small animal life buried beneath the ocean floor. My feet pedaled in slow motion, keeping me above him. Despite knowing the water was about 20 feet, the optical illusion told my brain the brown stingray was almost within touching distance.

He veered away from the rock, angling his body over the current, and moved his wings in broader strokes, increasing his speed to find new feeding grounds.

With my back toward the rock, I waited. My head raised as I checked my position in relation to the yacht. Rikki was still lying on the bow. She'd enjoyed the privacy and hadn't worn more than a pair of bikini bottoms since we started our search. Her comment was that she usually still had the captain and Sam on board, and such frivolities like nudity had to be constrained.

Constraining from anything seemed like an impossibility for her. She was one of those people who is so natural in their skin that the rest of the world could be damned. Rikki Talen did what she wanted, said what she wanted, and cared not one iota what someone else's opinion was of her. She wasn't selfish, though. So many people would consider her self-centered. That's not the case; she's confident, a trait that most people don't like in others, especially women.

My face plunged back into the water. A medium-sized grouper ambled across the sand. Unlike the ray, I could envision grilled grouper sandwiches, and my fins propelled me toward the bottom as I pulled the spear pole into position. When I was within range, I released my grip on the spear. A twang came off the rubber band attached to the end of the pole as the tension released. Three barbed spears at the other end struck the grouper just behind his gills. It wasn't an immediate kill, unfortunately, and the grouper attempted to dart away. As I pulled back, the fish on the end of the pole thrashed and fought to escape. The wound wasn't quite as sloppy as I thought. The fish just had a few seconds of fight in him. It twitched as I retrieved the spear.

An ominous shape appeared off in the distance–a juvenile bull shark. In the distance, he'd waited for me to bring down my prey, hoping to steal it from me. He wasn't big, but that didn't change how sharp his teeth were. I wasn't worried he would bite me on purpose. At least I hoped he wouldn't. I was too big of a threat to him. But in an attempt to steal my lunch and make it his own, those teeth might grab my arm instead.

Of course, I could have cut my losses, ripped the spear from the fish, and swam for the yacht. But grouper sandwiches are one of my favorite post-skin diving treats. And I would be damned if some punk kid, even if he was a shark, would try to best me for it.

He was moving steady and quick, but he was still at least 50 feet away. After kicking for the surface, I hoisted the spear pole out of the water, waving the dead grouper like it was a flag. It was an awkward position to swim in, keeping the grouper out of the water. My eyes stayed locked on the shark, and my feet propelled me to the boat.

When the grouper was no longer in the water, the shark sensed something was different. He slowed his approach. After a few seconds, boredom must have overtaken him, and he returned to his lurking along the sandy bottom.

Once he lost interest, I rolled all the way onto my back. It was an easier position to swim. The pole and fish remained out of the water. No point in tempting the juvenile to come take another look.

Rikki stood at the swim platform watching as I tossed the pole and fish onto the deck.

"What'd you get today?" she asked.

"Grouper. Almost had to fight a shark for the carcass though."

She lifted an eyebrow but said nothing.

"Anything on the monitors?" I asked, removing my mask.

"Yeah, it beeped once, and the camera found a piece of chain."

It was the same thing every day. The rover would eventually pinpoint something, and we'd check the cameras to find a chain, tin can, and once a tire rim. But no submarine. By now, I don't think it mattered to me. This was exactly what I would have been doing on *Carina*, only there would be no naked woman waiting to pounce on me every time I got back from snorkeling.

For Rikki, it might be different. She enjoyed this week of quiet simplicity, but there was something in her that found it boring. Or was going to find it boring. She needed an adventure, and this would not satisfy that need, no matter how much she enjoyed the freedom to make love anywhere on the boat.

"Is your shark friend gone?" she asked.

"Yeah, he lost interest."

She kissed me, biting my bottom lip gently before letting go. "I'm going for a swim."

With no splash, she dove into the clear water. Unable to contain my smile, I pulled the fins off my feet and carried my gear onto the aft deck. As I cleaned the fish, I gathered the scraps in a bucket. I didn't want to chum the surrounding waters, especially with that juvenile still in the area. So instead, I'd toss it all when we moved the boat again. That way nothing would get used to seeing the vessel and think it was dinner time.

I laid the filets out as I cut them off the fish and counted out seven thick pieces. It would be enough for lunch for two days. Might even have a snack.

Talitha has a big propane grill attached to the railing on the aft deck. Like everything else on the Nomad, it dwarfed my little round grill in *Carina's* cockpit. If I was the envious type, I'd be hard-pressed to go back to my Tartan after experiencing the comforts here. The thing is that the amenities come with a cost. For Rikki, it's minimal. She doesn't worry about money because her supply seems endless. The cost to maintain *Talitha* was 20 times what it cost me to keep *Carina* in tip-top shape. The fuel alone in this yacht ran $2,000 per fill-up. Mine was $50 to $70 tops. Hell, the refrigerator on board *Talitha* used more electricity in a day than everything I do in a week.

No, I can enjoy the luxury, but I remembered that somewhere someone is envious of my boat. So I'll stick with my freedom, but I'll gladly spend a week with Rikki anytime.

While the grill heated, I mixed up a quick marinade with apple cider vinegar, lime juice, shallots, and garlic. The grouper bathed in the marinade for 15 minutes while I cut up some tomatoes and romaine lettuce.

The grill sizzled when the filets hit the rack. My culinary opinion may not be widely accepted, but I hate it when the flesh dries out with fish. Too many overcook it, and the flavor gets lost. Unfortunately, that's often true of most meats. Fish takes very little time to cook, and it shouldn't be left alone. After about 45 seconds, I flipped each piece and drizzled the marinade over it. Less than a minute later, I plated the filets, squeezing a fresh lemon over them.

Rikki was floating on her back off the stern of the boat. I stared at her for a few seconds, and a smile came over my face. She was in her own universe at the moment. Zen-like.

"Want some lunch?" I shouted, breaking her serenity.

Her head lifted to look at me. Her body rotated, as if on an axis, as she righted herself in the water. She began stroking toward the platform, and I built our sandwiches. Hawaiian bread, grouper, lettuce, tomato, and sriracha mayonnaise.

I carried the plates aft and found her stretched out on the chaise lounge.

"I'm going to have to consider keeping you around," she suggested. "You might be too good for me."

"Nonsense," I explained, "I would do this if it were just me, so technically, you're just getting the by-product."

"Whatever," she grinned, "I'll take all the by-products you have to offer."

Halfway through my sandwich, an alarm sounded from the bridge.

"Looks like we got another hit," I commented.

"Maybe we found an anchor."

Laughing, I said, "That'd be nice. I need to add a backup to *Carina*."

Rikki started to get up, and I stopped her. "Finish your sandwich. I'll look."

I made my way to the bridge, carrying the rest of my lunch up the steps. The monitor for the rover was sitting on the nav station. The readings showed it was in 62 feet of water. I typed in a command with a few keystrokes, waiting as the underwater image on the screen adjusted. The rover rotated to widen the view.

A metal detection warning was still flashing as it turned. Even at that depth, the water was still crystal clear. The rover seemed to have come across some coral head. I widened the view more, commanding the rover to move. There was something unnatural about the reef. When I saw the conning tower, I released a gasp of excitement.

"Rikki!"

<h1 style="text-align:center">24</h1>

After confirming with Rikki that the image appeared to be a submarine, we hoisted our anchor and moved to the location that the rover was transmitting from. Exact coordinates came in from the unit's GPS, and it took us two hours to move to the site.

Anchoring *Talitha* in over 60 feet of water proved difficult. We dropped three anchors with extra rode so that the waves, wind, and current would have a tough time dragging her along the bottom. Once we were snug, we pulled the scuba gear out.

The U-boat appeared to be resting in a trench that ranged from 58 to 74 feet deep. Rampages from the sea had long ago begun its reclamation of the submarine. Tides and currents had over 80 years to shift the sandy bottom around the hull. Fan coral latched to the exterior, and barnacles were growing all along the steel skin.

At the depths we were diving, our bottom time was limited to 30 minutes before we had to come to the surface. Much longer than that, we would need to make a decompression stop on the way to the surface to allow the build-up of nitrogen to escape our system. Failure to pay attention to that can result in a case of the bends. Best to avoid the situation altogether for now.

Since this was an initial dive, there didn't seem to be any reason to drag it past half an hour. We could establish the condition of the hull and make some decisions about how we proceed safely inside.

After tightening the weight belt around my waist, I carried my fins and mask in one hand and the yellow BC and air cylinder in the other. Rikki followed me down the ladder to the swim platform. She opted to cover herself, putting on a bikini for the dive. She complained the inflatable vest would rub certain parts of her uncomfortably if she dove naked.

After sliding my arms into the BC, I cinched it tight around my chest. The weight of the tank attached to the vest forced me to lean forward slightly to compensate for the load. Rikki straightened up with her gear, stuck the air regulator in her mouth, pressed her right palm against the mask, and stepped backward into the water.

I followed Rikki and dropped into the water. Once in the water, I released a shot of air from my BC.

I reminded Rikki, taking the regulator out of my mouth, "We follow the anchor chain down and head north."

She gave me a thumbs up as she raised the valve above her head to release the air in her vest. We drifted toward the bottom, not wanting to drop too soon.

A silver chain hung below the hull, and I kept it in the corner of my left eye. Carbon dioxide bubbles from my lungs mixed with the bubbles of air gurgling out of the valve on my BC. Turning my head up, I watched the air, shaped like bulbous jellyfish, rush upward. *Talitha's* shape was distorted from below, the waves breaking up the surface like a fun-house mirror.

Once the air in my vest was gone, I continued my downward drift. Lead weights on my belt helped carry me down; otherwise, my body would try to float to the surface automatically. Rikki waved off the weights, telling me she was a sinker, and once gravity took hold, she would drop to the bottom like a stone.

When I glanced down, I saw she was already ten feet deeper than I was and still slowly letting air out of her BC. Leveling my body, I floated toward the bottom. As I twisted even more, my head angled down, and I pedaled my fins, propelling me down a little faster.

Despite attempting to speed my descent, I reached the bottom several seconds after Rikki. She added air from her cylinder into her vest to hold her a foot or so above the bottom. My depth gauge stated it was 54 feet, and it appeared we were on a slope leading into the trench where the sub was resting.

We performed a basic check, which comprised each of us flashing the "Okay" sign with our hands followed by a thumbs up. As I pointed down the slope, I directed Rikki to take the lead. While we had never done a dive together, I was confident that she was more than capable like everything else she did. Nonetheless, I wanted to put her in the lead for now. If we could have talked, I'd have commented how following her only let me check out her ass as she swam. Of course, that was just an added benefit.

Truthfully, I like a certain amount of control in a situation. As the leader of our unit in Afghanistan, I developed a habit of ensuring that I knew where my men were at all times. It's an impossible task that required me to trust that they were going to be there. Rikki had the same amount of courage that most of my guys did, but she lacked discipline. She'd been playing solo too long to understand the need for cohesion.

Maybe I was needlessly anal about it. Since one of us had to take the lead, it didn't hurt that it was her.

The trench angled deeper, and a thought occurred to me. Had the U-boat created the groove when it struck the bottom?

The mound ahead resembled a reef, except for its uniformity. Another few years would allow the coral and sea life to camouflage the rest of the structure. The rounded edges were still distinguishable. The explosion appeared to peel the steel hull back. We were staring at the bow and the breach caused by Adams and his crafty sabotage.

The hole in the metal hull was ten feet long, angling diagonally along the side. The fissure was only about two feet wide. Metal was flaking away from the edges as the salt devoured the alloy. A buckle formed in the steel, and initially, the rupture was likely not as wide. However, at a 60 foot depth, the size of the fracture only affected how long until the vessel filled with sea water.

There would not be much room for us to slip through the crack with our cylinders strapped to our back. However, we did anticipate cutting into the hull, and I obtained a torch designed for this type of underwater work. It would widen the opening enough for one of us to slip through.

I motioned for Rikki to move along the hull, wanting to check for any other hull breaches. Once we got inside, we might find our exploration hampered by sealed compartments. Any other openings might allow us to access different sections of the submarine from the outside.

Throughout my dive career I had several opportunities to dive both new and old wrecks. I knew that the most dangerous thing was becoming trapped inside the vessel. The sea was an unfriendly place to anything that wasn't natural to it, and it would ravage a foreign object. Bulkheads might be unstable, and just the motion a diver creates in the water could send the structure crumbling down.

If time was an easy commodity, I preferred to take the salvage one step at a time.

Rikki's fins turned down, halting her. A swift kick guided me over to her, where I could see a moray slinking in and out of a small round shaft in the sub. The green eel's mouth opened and closed, revealing the tiny sharp teeth. He menaced us for disrupting his area, but he was no threat.

We'd been down for 16 minutes. We had less than that to cover the exterior of the boat. As I nudged Rikki, I tapped my wrist before directing her to continue aft. She nodded her understanding and pedaled her fins. Satisfied that we were sufficiently frightened, the eel retreated into its sanctuary.

The conning tower rose ahead of us. A surreality of the familiar shape hit me. This was a tomb, and despite the side of the war the men on board fought, they were still men. All were sons of mothers who may have never known what happened to them. Fathers and brothers. Their bodies were long since gone, but this was still a graveyard.

After adjusting my attitude in the water, I swam up to the hatch atop the tower. Despite knowing full well it wouldn't budge, I attempted to turn the wheel. Oxidation jammed the gears. The only thing that seemed to move was the bits of rust flakes I scraped off the metal. The hull was intact, but with the gouging torch, I might be able to cut it open, allowing another point of entry.

Another six minutes had passed, and we reached the tail of the U-boat. Any markings that had been on the hull had long since faded with the current. The rest of the hull remained intact.

The explosion was forward, buckling the hull and flooding the forward compartment. No doubt the sudden surge of water would alter the attitude of the submarine, pitching it forward. The crew might not have had time to attempt to surface, depending on the extent of the internal damage.

Our time was almost up, and I motioned for Rikki to follow me. We should be able to make it back to the anchor chain in under five minutes. When I crested the top of the trench, the flat bottom opened up. I glided over the sand, letting my fingers drag through the grains as I kicked. The bits flittered up in the water like tiny flocks of birds before settling back with their brothers.

The plow anchor was dug into the sand just ahead. Tiny shrimp were pecking at the metal, picking off microscopic organisms. The chain stretched out in the sand for 15 feet before beginning a slow rise toward the surface.

Rikki swam up beside me as I checked our time. We were just within our 30 minute time. Pointing toward the surface, I indicated it was time to head up. She offered a thumbs up, smiling through her regulator.

When I pressed the button on my BC, the air from the cylinder on my back filled the vest's bladder slowly. An ascension from any depth has to be gradual. The water pressure on the body is greater down deep, and a speedy ascent can cause problems. While rising off the bottom, I kept my eyes down. It's childish, but watching me lift off the ocean floor gives me this sense of flight. There's a lifting of my spirit in that moment.

After a few seconds, my eyes turned toward the surface. The air in the BC was increasing my speed. The last ten feet always feel like I'm rocketing up, and when I break through the surface, I bounce for a second before bobbing in the water. As I turned around, I established my bearings. The world is different above water.

The water next to me bubbled for a second as Rikki popped up. She spat the regulator out of her mouth, still grinning.

"We found it," she exhaled with panting excitement. She'd been waiting half an hour to tell me something I was obviously there to see.

With a grin, I nodded. "Let's get back on board."

She rolled onto her back, kicking toward the stern of *Talitha*. After waiting a second for her to get a head start, I followed her. As I grabbed the platform, I righted myself in the water, uncinched the BC, and slipped out of it. While I climbed onto the platform, Rikki held my inflated vest and cylinder.

While I hauled both sets of gear onto the boat, I let Rikki push herself up on the deck. Her dark skin dripped, and I watched a particular bead of water make a luge run off her shoulder and down her cleavage.

"My eyes are up here," she joked.

"Sorry," I muttered, "Cave man instincts kicked in."

She reached behind her back and unclipped the bikini top. She tossed it onto the aft deck, almost snarling. "Let's see those instincts."

25

The arc was almost impossible to see. I didn't want to see it though. It was a tiny blue bolt of electricity, and if I didn't work with diligence, the arc might leap from the metal I was cutting to the salt water around me. Nothing about the possibility of being boiled to death sounded like fun. I'm sure some more experienced salvage consultant would explain in unequivocal terms that the odds of that happening were nonexistent. However, when I went through the training with a Naval demolition expert, it was the one thing he said that sent shivers through me.

Because of Corporal James, the lingering thought of becoming a crispy Chase stayed in my forethought as I drew a slow line from the bulging fissure on the nose of the submarine. This kind of work was lonely–the only sound was the sizzle that the arc made as it gouged through the steel. But of course, the sizzling sound didn't detract from the thought of being boiled alive.

The arc gouger we brought with us required someone on the boat to operate it while I worked underwater. Since

I at least had the training the U.S. government thought necessary, I was the obvious choice for the underwater work. Unfortunately, we didn't have radios like most salvage crews would, forcing us to adopt more primitive communication methods. A rope hooked to my BC that ran along the arc gouger's tube to the *Talitha* in this case. There it threaded its way through a block pulley and attached to a bell. Once we realized we didn't have the set up for me to talk to her from the ocean floor, we decided to MacGyver something workable.

Since I was the one running the risk of cooking, the contraption worried me. It should be simple. I descend to the ocean floor with the arc gouger and line. Once I'm in place and ready to cut, I pull the rope four times hard. We wait precisely 15 seconds, and Rikki gives me four sharp tugs in response. Because I was overly cautious, I would respond another 15 seconds later with four more pulls. At that point, Rikki would count another 15 seconds and power up the arc gouger.

The extra time should allow me to get into position before she started the machine. When I finished cutting, I would give four more pulls. There was no added response time. Anything from me would result in an immediate shutdown.

So far, the system was working. I was not crispy, and the steel hull was peeling back in slow layers. My attention was so intent on the end of the tube connecting to the submarine's skin that a sexy mermaid could have pulled up behind me on a seahorse without my seeing it.

The plan was to use my 30 minutes of bottom time to cut the fissure wide enough for me to get inside on the next dive and explore the interior. The rope would remain attached to me even as I made my entry into the U-boat, in case Rikki had to come in to find me.

There were still 10 minutes on the clock before I had to begin my ascent–no point in rushing. Either I finished it during this dive or returned to the boat, waited about an hour, and then completed the work. At the rate I was cutting, there would be a significant gap in the hull in the remaining time.

A rectangular chunk of metal broke free, dropping to the bottom. I trimmed the opening more by moving the tip around, ensuring that there weren't too many jagged edges to snag an air hose or rip a BC. Next to cooking to death, suffocating was high on my list of things to avoid.

The round bubbles of hot steel would instantly solidify and rain down beneath me. My hand reached for my rope and jerked it four times. Three to four seconds passed, and the cutting ceased. Relaxing, I peered into the hole. I had three minutes before I needed to start my ascent.

Despite knowing I would be back in an hour, curiosity got the better of me. After unclipping my flashlight from my BC, I shone the beam into the submarine. Twisted metal stared back at me. The initial explosion reshaped the metal stringers and beams. Decades of salt water marred them more. Now it looked like some post-modern sculpture that someone would tell me emotes the struggle between something or another.

Through the gnarled tangle of metal, an opening appeared to lead aft. My heart pounded as I considered swimming deeper into the tomb.

Since I knew time was limited, I pushed my head back out of the hole. No point in going forward. Time to head back to the surface.

With one hand guiding me up the rope to the boat, I rose gradually. Rikki stood at the rear of the watercraft retrieving the arc gouger as I came out of my BC.

"Get it clear?" she asked, leaning over to drag my BC onto the boat.

"Yeah, I should be good," I explained as I pulled up on to the platform. Once I stripped my fins off, I stood up and arched my back in a stretch.

"I whipped up some conch salad if you want some lunch."

My stomach barked when it heard there was food. Scuba diving and snorkeling had that effect on me. I would come back from a dive hungry and in need of a nap. Both of which seemed like a good idea at the moment.

Rikki padded off while I pulled the neoprene boots off my feet and flopped on the chaise lounge. The warm tropic sun dried the droplets on my chest. My arm draped across my eyes, shielding them from the rays of the sun.

Footfalls broke my meditation, and I sat up as Rikki passed a plate with a quarter of a French baguette sliced longways and filled with conch salad. She swore the salad was her own making. The conch was fresh from the sea floor yesterday. The mango and oranges she diced were picked up in Bimini.

Both hands scooped up the bread as I devoured it. When I was sated, I lay back on the chaise and drifted off to sleep.

"Chase," Rikki roused me from my nap after a few minutes.

Once I sat up and blinked a few times, I checked my watch. An hour had passed since I came up from the wreck–time for me to take another dive. There was still enough time in the day for me to make a few more exploratory dives.

"Sorry," I mumbled as I started hooking up my gear.

"Don't apologize," she told me. "You're the one doing all the heavy lifting today."

My hand grabbed her waist as I dragged her into my lap. She cupped her hands around my face and kissed me. My hands slid down her hips.

"Save that for later," she whispered in my ear before jumping to her feet.

"I'm going to recon a bit," I told her. "If I need to use the cutter, I'll come back up for it."

"I'll be manning the deck for you," she smiled as I climbed down onto the swim platform.

Rikki tossed me the end of the rope to clip to my belt. "Just in case," she warned.

Nodding, I attached the line to my vest and stepped into the water.

As I sank below the surface, I felt my chest pumping with excitement. Every kid I knew imagined going on a treasure hunt. My sister and I dug holes around the woods in our neighborhood searching for a legendary trove of Aztec gold. At the time, the concept that Arkansas was a little off the beaten path for the average Aztec wasn't comprehensible to an 11-year-old. Now, I was about to get the first glimpse inside this time capsule. It was surreal. The anticipation. The glory. I was Indiana Jones. And fortune and glory were just below me.

The opening into the nose of the U-boat stared at me. With my light in my right hand, I hooked my left on the jagged edge and pulled myself into the submarine.

Sunlight that easily filtered through the crystal clear waters extinguished as soon as I entered. Like the whale, the hull of the boat swallowed me as if I was Jonah. My light shined about the compartment. Twisted metal stooped over me. Even though I knew that there was no chance of finding the corpses of the German Naval officers, that knowledge didn't soothe the expectation that it might happen. The dead are a part of life, and I'd seen more than my fair share of corpses. Some had been the result of my own actions. The thought of finding the dead here was otherworldly. Ghostly.

Shivers ran down my spine as I considered the death that these men endured. Trapped for hours or even days, knowing that the end was closing in on them. That's not high on my list of ways to die.

The force of the explosion had not only mangled the structure of the compartment and torn a breach in the hull–forward ballast tanks were obliterated. Submarines would rise and dive based on the air pumped into those tanks. When the torpedoes detonated, the tanks filled with water, pushing the nose of the sub into a dive that drove it into the sea floor.

My light splayed across an open hatch as I swam aft. A steel door hung from one hinge. As I proceeded forward, I maneuvered through the door. The next compartment was narrow and crowded. Metal framed bunk beds lined the walls. The platforms of rusted wire were disintegrating with only a few strands winding between the frame–crew quarters.

I pulled some slack in the rope hooked to my vest, not wanting to snag on any of the openings. The next hatch was open still. The aftermath of Rusty Adams must have been chaotic and fast. As soon as the hull ruptured, crew-men should have been sealing hatches to slow the slew of water gushing into the ship.

After moving through that hatch, I found myself in what had been the command center. The conning tower was above me, and a ladder rose into the dark hole over-head. The instrument panels, long since darkened, were intact and near museum pieces. They could be salvaged and put on display in no time.

It wasn't a task that interested me. There was a conflict in my head between salvaging the gold and preserving the wreck. Were we disrupting the dead? Did we have the right to do that?

A hatch in the floor was sealed. Both hands gripped the handle as I attempted to open it. It didn't budge. Toward the rear of the command compartment, a sealed door locked me out of the aft sections. This was as far as this foray would take me without the arc gouger.

Only 13 minutes had passed. I could return to the surface for a brief break and come back with the cutter. Two
more dives should get me deeper into the belly of the tomb.

26

I should have known better. Two more dives turned into four, and by the time I surfaced exhaustion set in and I'd only gotten the hatches on the conning tower and the deck cut open. Finally, the hard work resulted in access into the battery room beneath the command center.

Rikki was drooling at the idea of taking her own tour of the U-boat. When I pulled myself up on the platform, she already donned her gear.

"I'm just taking a look," she promised as she unhooked the line from my BC and connected it to hers.

Nodding, I didn't have the energy to argue with her. She'd spent the entire day on the boat, and she wasn't about to miss seeing what she had been hunting.

"Be careful," I warned. "I cut the bottom hatch free, but it's a tight fit."

"I'll just stick my head in," she confirmed before dropping back into the water.

As she sank below the surface, I dragged my cylinder over to the compressor, attaching the hoses to it before flipping the switch. The motor roared to life, sputtering as it began refilling the air. The afternoon had slipped past, with me spending the majority in a dark hole. Watching the gauges, my eyes locked on the quivering needle as it climbed up. When it reached about 1,500 psi, I cut the motor off and disconnected the hoses. The aluminum cylinder was cold to the touch. I hoisted it onto my shoulder before carrying it over and latching it into the cubby with three other tanks.

As soon as I plopped down on the chaise lounge, I felt the muscles in my arms tremble. Before diving on the sub, I found a basic schematic of a German U-boat. It wouldn't be accurate, but it would give me a basis for exploring the wreck.

The aft hatch should lead to an engine room and, I hoped, the stowage area. That left only a space left to explore, but I didn't think I had it in me for another dive today. My last dive gave me a head start on cutting through the rear hatch. Both hinges were loose, and only the lever secured the hatch.

Another ten minutes passed before I heard the wheezing bubbles of Rikki's ascent. She shredded her BC before I reached the stern of the boat. My fingers clasped the handle at the top of the back support as I hoisted the gear onto the vessel.

"I can't believe it," she hissed as she gracefully popped up onto the back of the boat. "It's insane."

After sliding down, I dropped my feet into the water next to her.

"The instruments," she gasped, pulling her fins off. "They look perfect."

Nodding, I took her fins and mask and tossed them up onto the aft deck.

She continued, "Can you imagine what those men must have gone through? That front compartment is a mess."

"Anyone in there would have been killed instantly," I pointed out somberly.

"Yeah," she whispered.

"I don't know about you," I observed, "but I think I could go for something to eat and a few hours to just unwind. Tomorrow morning will start us all over again."

"I have to say," Rikki commented, "I've done some crazy shit, hunting down relics and treasures, but this has been the most fun."

"That's my motto."

She leaned over and kissed me. "Gosh," I pined with feigned bashfulness. "You're real sweet."

"Come on," she goaded, "let's make dinner."

As the evening sun dipped below the horizon, we lounged on the upper deck, the blood-red sky stretched around us as the purple night pushed against the daylight. The rum and pineapple juice in my glass was gone, and Rikki lay curled up under my arm. A breeze brought goosebumps on her arm. I reached around her and pulled the beach blanket over us. Her steady breathing against my chest comforted me.

When I awoke the night was dark. Lights on the lower decks cast a soft glow out onto the water, but they didn't dilute the night sky. Stars shone bright, and the Milky Way glowed like a marked trail over the world. The clock in my head guessed it was around two in the morning.

Somewhere I heard a low hum, and I searched the sky for a plane running a red-eye schedule across the Atlantic.

Rikki continued to breathe softly, and my eyes closed again.

The splashing woke me, and I peered over the rail at three dolphins that were playing just off the hull. When I stood up, Rikki stirred.

"We slept here all night?" she mumbled.

Pointing at the dolphins, I told her, "Our wake-up crew has arrived."

"Did they bring coffee?" she asked in jest, barely opening her eyes to register the creatures.

Laughing, I promised, "Five minutes, and I'll be back with a cup."

"Cream and sugar."

An hour later, I swam back through the conning tower hatch. Ten minutes after I started, the latch on the door fell loose. The years of rust still braced it in place. With some effort and a makeshift pry bar, I wedged the hatch open. The hatch inched forward before breaking free of the rusted seal.

Muffled clanging of the door on the steel deck reverberated through the compartment. On the other side of the hatch stood a small room with controls everywhere. Radio room, I guessed. Unfortunately, most of the outer facade of the equipment had deteriorated. The wooden panels were only bits of saturated pulp, and the fibrous cords had frayed to only thin copper lines.

At the rear of the room, another door hung open. After kicking through the door, I found myself in the engine room. The diesel engine, which filled a quarter of the room, had a thin coat of a slimy rust or a rusty slime. I dragged my fingers over the slime, leaving a trail.

The engine was a giant. The diesel on *Carina* was only 20 hp. I had no idea what this one was. It would have taken a lot of power to move the behemoth through the water. Despite the size of the engine, there was still ample room to swim around the engine room. Tools were scattered about the deck while some wrenches still hung on racks as if the crew just returned them.

I could have studied the layout of all the levers, valves, and pipes for hours. There just wasn't time for it. I had another 20 minutes on this dive.

Behind the motor, a ladder rose from below the deck. I turned my body to climb down the ladder upside down. Below the engine lay another bank of batteries along with a stack of boxes.

My chest pounded hard enough so that I could hear the pulse in my ears. Was I looking at the gold we had been hunting? A quick count came up with 22.

The boxes were metal, and when I lifted one up, the handle on one side snapped off. My arms scooped up the box, and I swam back up the ladder. The steel crate weighed about 30 pounds. It was difficult to be exact, but it didn't feel like 50 pounds, though, like Jacob Altman said.

My brain started doing the math. It's inevitable; the figuring and counting. It's why people start imagining how they would spend a lottery win before the ticket is even bought. The human threshold for dreaming is limitless.

So I multiplied as I carried my treasure aft. I counted 22 cases that weighed 30 pounds each. 660 pounds. Of course, the box would weigh three to five pounds. Subtract about 100 pounds. 560 pounds of gold. If the crates contained all coins, and the coins weighed an ounce each, the box I carried should have roughly 480 coins. Rikki suggested each coin could be worth $30, meaning I held $14,400 in my hand.

Or I could open it to find a case of submarine parts. But until I reached the surface, the box was, as Bogie described it, "the stuff that dreams were made of."

I continued forward until I reached the control room where I swam up and through the hatch on the conning tower. Once I was back in the open ocean, I inflated my BC and drifted upward. The box was tightly nestled in my arms.

I imagined Henry Richman clinging to his box in the water. It would have been a feat after several days. The crate was bulky but manageable. Once I reached the surface though, the waves and current would make it increasingly difficult to hold onto. Especially for days on end.

My head broke the surface just off the stern. Rikki wasn't on deck. After twisting onto my back, I pedaled my fins propelling me backward.

When I bumped into the swim platform, I turned and heaved the metal crate onto the back.

"Rikki!" I shouted, uncinching the buckle holding my BC tight around my chest.

Once I climbed on board, I carried the box onto the aft deck.

"Rikki!"

The box was secured by two knobs that twisted to pull the lip around the lid tight. Unfortunately, the knobs had rusted tight from the years underwater. After retrieving a pair of channel lock pliers from the toolbox next to the air compressor, I broke the rusted seal.

The lid opened, and I held my breath as I stared at the gold coins filling the box. A smile grew across my face as I exhaled.

"Rikki!" I rose to find her.

Two men came out of the door leading to the galley. I froze, studying them. I recognized two of the bikers we ran into at the bar. Both held small H&K MP7s with suppressors which were meant to look more menacing than to silence them.

A gray haired man stepped out between the two. He was dressed like he should have been on a golf course in West Palm. Linen pants and shirt with muted pastel colors. His dark brown skin had the kind of seamless color that requires a daily regime in a tanning bed.

My brain needed a second to match his face. He was older than the picture I had seen on the book's dust jacket in Paul Richman's house. Daniel Wexler, neo-Nazi extraordinaire.

Reflexes caused me to do a double-take. I didn't see another boat tied up to *Talitha*. I never heard a motor, but I could have missed it while I was inside the submarine.

"Where's Rikki?" I demanded.

"Is that my gold?" he hissed. His voice was an octave higher than I'd have imagined. He enunciated each phonetic as he spoke.

"I don't think so," I snarled. Hairs on my neck stood on end, and I felt my body shift into fight mode.

Both bikers leveled their guns at me. The bushy bearded one I hit with the Coors Light bottle narrowed his eyes at me–a warning light of sorts.

"Mr. Gordon," Wexler's incipient voice broke the trance. "There's no need to get your hackles up. I don't want to hurt you."

"The hell you don't," I snapped.

Wexler glanced over his shoulder at the other biker. "Tell Mike to bring the black bitch up here."

Every scenario I ran left me riddled with bullets. There was no way I could cover the distance between Bushy Beard and me before he pulled the trigger. The MP7 could fire over 900 rounds a minute, but that was moot. There were only about 20 in the mag, which would be more than enough to Swiss cheese me.

Rikki stumbled out of the door with Bushy Beard gripping her arm.

"Mr. Gordon," Wexler continued, "here's what's going to happen. You are going to dive down and retrieve all the gold. If you don't, I'll shoot you and Miss Talen here and get it myself."

"What happens once I get the gold up here?"

"I promise I won't shoot either of you," he vowed.

Empty promise. There was little chance he wouldn't kill us. The only thing it bought me was time.

"It'll take several dives."
"You have one."

27

There was no chance that retrieving 22 steel boxes from the belly of the U-boat was going to be accomplished in my half hour time limit. I wasn't sure I'd be able to finish it all on one tank of air. However, Wexler wasn't concerned with my well-being. He intended to prod me with the barrel of Bushy Beard's H&K pressed against Rikki's head.

There wasn't a way to add two tanks to my back. We didn't have the correct gear. I could change cylinders on the bottom. It wasn't a difficult task. In fact, it was one of the first safety training drills I learned.

The issue wasn't the air. It was all about nitrogen. The human body isn't designed to be underwater for long periods of time. We as a race see that more as a challenge. As long as I was stayed down for less than 30 minutes, my body wasn't absorbing too much nitrogen. In truth, I could have stretched my time longer with a decompression stop.

The decompression stop is done at shallower depths. The body will release the nitrogen slowly, allowing the diver to spend several minutes at 15 to 20 feet before continuing the ascension. Divers that stay too long in deeper waters absorb lots of nitrogen, and that can cause nitrogen narcosis. A fun little effect that can cause hallucinations and eventually death.

The second biker lowered the metal platform into the water to retrieve the gold. Two cables attached to the winches on the davits hanging over the transom. The metal platform sank as the winches fed out more line.

"The sooner you get this done," Wexler advised, "the sooner we can get on our way."

With a scowl directed at him, I carried my gear and the extra cylinder to the swim platform. Wexler had another man with him who stood about midship. He was there to make sure I didn't attempt to re-board the vessel. Where he stood would make it difficult to get on board without his seeing me.

With the extra cylinder in my hand, I stepped off the platform. The last thing I saw was Rikki's eyes. The look was a promise of sorts. I wasn't done yet.

Once I reached the bottom, I had limited time. There was no point in tying the line to me. No one was going to save me if I ran into trouble. The extra cylinder rested on the sandy bottom next to the platform. I kicked toward the trench.

The most efficient move was to get all the boxes out of the cargo hold first and through the conning tower hatch. Once I made my way deep into the U-boat, I began hauling boxes.

The timer in my head was clicking away. It took me one minute and six seconds to pick up the box, swim it up the ladder and through the radio room and control center, and set it on the conning tower. Another 42 seconds to make the swim back to the cargo hold.

While the seconds clicked away, I wondered how Wexler found us. How did he get on board? There weren't any other boats around? I considered Richman's de Havilland. He could have landed and dropped off Wexler and his men. They'd be hard pressed to sneak up on Rikki, though.

Something about her demeanor told me she was surprised. Like I was. Too surprised to fight. It happened too quickly, and that bothered me.

My fourth trip. I'd passed ten minutes of bottom time and hadn't scratched the surface. Worse, I still didn't know what I was going to do to get us out of this. The disadvantage was all on me. I was in the water and unarmed.

One thing at a time, I urged myself.

The only way I was going to finish was by taking two boxes at a time. Unfortunately, the added weight made maneuvering through the hatches difficult, almost two minutes from the cargo hold to the conning tower.

Six more trips emptied the cargo hold. I had been down for almost 45 minutes. The exertion of carrying the extra weight had me breathing harder and using far too much air. The needle on my air gauge said I was at 400 psi. As a general rule, I try to head to the surface when my air gets that low.

With two boxes in my arms, I added some air to my BC to help lift me out of the trench. Then, kicking toward the boat, I hauled the boxes over and started stacking them on the metal platform.

My air was at 390 psi. It was a chance, but I pushed it for a few more trips.

Three more trips from the sub to the platform left me at 290 psi. If the gauge wasn't calibrated, I could find myself sucking an empty tank. To change cylinders, I had to take off the BC, turn off the cylinder, remove the regulator, and reattach it to the new tank. The entire process took less than a minute, and like I said, it was part of the basic safety training.

As I slipped out of my BC, I kept my regulator in my mouth. With one deep breath, I twisted the knob to stop the flow of air. A different knob was required to remove the regulator. Half a minute later, I had the regulator attached to the full cylinder and the air flowing to my lungs.

56 minutes of bottom time. Off the top of my head, I was confident that I required about 30 minutes of decompression at this point.

Time to get moving. Over the next ten minutes, I made six more trips back and forth before I stacked all the gold on the platform. After setting the empty cylinder next to the gold, I prepared to make my ascent. My total bottom time was an hour and seven minutes. I would need close to 40 minutes at 20 feet–something I thought Wexler wasn't likely to give me.

When I reached 20 feet, I leveled off and started the timer on my watch. I had 900 psi still in the tank, and if I maintained steady breathing it should last me 40 minutes.

Waiting is never my strong suit. One would think I was better at it. The Corps spent a lot of time training me to "hurry up and wait." It makes me nervous. Too much to consider while in neutral. I consider myself a man of action or, more often than not, a man of reaction. When things are moving, I don't have time to think about the options. Generally, I pick the right one. At least I've survived all the encounters thus far. I must have chosen wisely.

Move forward. It's almost a motto. And at this moment, I wasn't moving anywhere. Just over 20 feet above me, Rikki was held hostage, and I couldn't do anything. I'd made too many repeated dives throughout the last two days to risk not making a decompression stop. I'd be useless if the nitrogen in my blood expanded and started rupturing blood vessels or worse.

Just stay calm.

I didn't. Any calm I was mustering escaped when the metal platform began clicking as it rose from the ocean floor. I knew what was happening. Wexler had no plans to let me re-board *Talitha*. If I didn't do something, Rikki and I would find ourselves in a worse situation.

"Shit," I cursed into my regulator. All I could hear was the burst of bubbles.

The platform passed me. They still had to secure the gold. That would take a few minutes.

After checking my watch, I knew it wouldn't be enough. I had 34 minutes before I could safely surface. My ears strained to listen for movement as I saw the seconds tick around the face of the watch. They were slower than usual.

If I returned to the bottom, would I be able to drag the 45 pound plow anchor toward the submarine? We should have dropped enough chain. If the anchor was secured, Wexler wouldn't be able to raise it. Then, of course, I'd be forced to start my decompression all over.

No, I needed another option. Right now, it was just waiting.

After about 10 minutes, the stern anchor chain began retracting. I was out of time. I'd been down around 17 minutes. It would take another minute or two to stow the rear anchor. Maybe two to three minutes to hoist the main anchor. I'd only be halfway through my decompression.

My eyes closed. I was fit and strong. If I could hold off a few more minutes before rising, there was a chance that if I got decompression sickness, it would only be a mild case. Still nothing to scoff at, but with luck not life threatening.

Better than being dead. Worse yet, seeing them kill Rikki.

The stern anchor rose past me. If I could only buy some minutes. After kicking toward the anchor, I caught it in my arms and swam under the boat. I swam under the hull of the vessel and tossed the anchor around the starboard propeller before sinking back down a few feet.

The propeller was still seven feet under water, and I hoped the quick ascension to that depth hadn't caused me any issues. The grinding of metal on metal echoed through the water.

For the next four minutes, I watched the chain tense and loosen as they tried to pull the anchor free. Something unexpected happened. The splash of water from above signaled someone entering the water. Rikki?

No, the second biker. He swam along the stainless-steel chain about 12 feet above me. The idiot wasn't wearing a mask. He was told to go clear the propeller, and he just obeyed.

Unsheathing the dive knife from my calf, I moved under him. My fins shot me upward. My free hand caught him by the shirt and pulled him down. The knife entered just under his ribs. The blade should have pierced through the liver. I pushed myself back down again, dragging him with me.

Panic set in as he tried to thrash away. Red leaked out of him like streamers at a party. His hand, still gripping the anchor chain, pulled the links off the propeller. The weight of the anchor swung toward the stern of the boat, jerking him out of my hand. He struggled for the surface, but the blood loss had weakened him. The fight he put up only allowed the knife to tear his liver apart.

From several feet away, I saw the life seep out of his eyes. The anchor climbed toward the boat and disappeared through the distorted surface.

My stop had been 26 minutes, assuming the two quick ascents had caused no issues. A quick self-assessment told me I was still thinking clearly. There didn't appear to be any side effects.

The shadow on the ocean floor caught my eye. It was moving from the trench toward me.

Another bull shark. This one wasn't a juvenile either. He rose off the sandy bottom and circled me and the dead biker.

This fellow was a male. He was a little over six feet long, from the tip of his tail to his snout.

My feet backpedaled toward the bow of the boat. I wanted to give the boy plenty of room with the dead Nazi. Just in case, I turned the knife into a striking position and waited for him to come past me.

The bow anchor vibrated as the windlass cranked the chain into the anchor locker–time for me to go. I was pushing 30 minutes, and with the new arrival, I decided to chance decompression sickness. My free hand caught the chain, and I let my feet rest on the rising anchor.

The sound of the chain grinding changed as my weight added to the line. I hoped the boys up top wouldn't pay attention.

The bull shark struck, flying in and tearing into the corpse's arm. Clouds of red exploded from the body. Wincing, I held the blade, ready to attack as I neared the surface.

The engines rumbled to life, and I peered up the chain. My head broke the surface. Water streamed off the glass on my mask.

"There!" someone shouted.

I saw the barrel of the H&K raise up. Falling back, I struck the water as a slew of bullets exploded from the gun.

After dropping my knife, I caught the cinch on my BC and released it. The inflatable vest came off as I dove under the boat. The cylinder pulled the now-deflated BC toward the ocean floor. With a push off the bottom of the boat, I turned to swim toward the stern.

Ahead, the mutilated corpse hung ten feet below the surface in a cloud of blood. There was no sign of the bull shark, but I doubted he was gone. With a high-pitched whine, the propellers started turning, and I dove a little deeper. The wash from the propellers pushed the corpse down as the vessel moved away.

When I came up behind it, I churned my fins hard toward the swim platform, only a few feet above me. My body lunged out of the water as the platform passed a few feet from me.

Bushy Beard stood on the aft deck, aiming his MP7 toward me. I sank below the surface as it spat out a blast of rounds.

28

Talitha retreated from me, and I didn't have much time to watch her leave. My feet pushed me deeper, avoiding the bullets slicing through the sea. After resurfacing, I caught a glimpse of Bushy Beard laughing off the stern rail of the yacht. Despite a burning urge to attempt to give chase, my attention shifted as a fin sliced through the water less than 20 feet from me.

Diving below the surface, I located the bull shark circling his meal. Unfortunately for me, I was inside that path, some place I didn't want to stay for any length of time.

My head popped up out of the water to get my bearing. The yacht sped away at about ten knots. For the time being, I had to forget about Rikki. She was on her own. If I didn't survive, there would be little I could do for her anyhow.

Get away from the shark bait, Chase.

I dropped my head into the water and caught the snorkel in my mouth and began a slow, steady track north. No splashing or quick movements. Just a non-threatening retreat.

The bull shark made a wide arc around the dead body, and as he swam on the southern half of his meandering pass, I kept going north.

He passed me again. Only ten feet away. His beady eyes seemed to ignore me, but I knew better. More likely those eyes assessed me. Threat? Prey? I didn't want to be either.

Despite the fear-inspiring ferocity that he tore into the biker, he magnified beauty. In almost any other circumstance, I'd be filled with awe at the powerful muscles that moved him so gracefully through the water. However, he exhibited no effort in his movement. Instead, his tail swiped in tiny motions and propelled him forward, while his pectoral fins angled in and out to adjust his heading.

However, at the moment, I couldn't enjoy the awe of the creature. It wasn't fear coursing through me, either. Apprehension, perhaps. Certainly, a healthy, leaning toward a heavy, amount of respect. But not fear. That wasn't going to help me at this point. Survival required me to move forward, or at least away from the beast.

The next time he came around, he cut between me and his meal. I didn't breathe a sigh of relief yet. My feet continued to push me away without making any splashes on the surface.

When I put a hundred yards between us, I rolled onto my back and searched among the waves. The movement of the dorsal fin caught my eye in the distance. The creature stayed with his food, and I hoped he would be completely satisfied by the meal for a bit. As long as I moved away, I should present no threat to him.

A dull throb developed just behind my eyes. It could have been a mild case of the bends or simple dehydration. There wasn't much I could do here. I needed to find rescue or it wouldn't matter.

Rusty Adams found himself in the same situation. His solution was to swim north to Andros Island. It seemed as good a plan as any.

As long as I had a plan, I felt better. Until the worry about Rikki settled in. What was Wexler going to do with her?

Just swim. Worry later.

Andros lay roughly 30 miles north. I could cover a mile an hour, in prime conditions more. A swimmer whose name I will never remember swam over 100 miles in less than two days. I'd be lucky to cover the 30 miles in the same amount of time.

She had an escort boat, too. How else can you record those world records? They are all lies, I'm sure. The actual world record is held by someone with no escort, lost at sea, and desperately seeking survival. It doesn't matter if you blow past the world record if you never make it to shore. There are no photographs by Guinness. The only recognition might be an obituary or, if you're lucky, a news article about your disappearance.

My brain switched gears. A Guinness would be good right now, but I'd settle for some shitty light beer right now.

Focus, Chase. No point in losing track.

Andros is a big island, I reminded myself. Keep pointing northeast. Just not too far northeast. Florida would be another 50 or 60 miles.

The next few hours passed slowly. My feet never slowed, and I made no attempts to break any speed records. I just wanted to make it to shore in one piece.

My brain worked as I cut through the water. Make it to shore first. Then, Wexler. I had every intention of killing him. That thought pushed me forward.

After six hours, I rolled onto my back. The afternoon sun stretched as it began to set. The sky burned orange, and I floated on my back, watching the colors transform the firmament as I rested for a few minutes.

A short break. That's all I allowed myself. A few minutes to rest my legs before continuing on. The thought that I might be wasting daylight crossed my mind. I dismissed it. I was going to swim well into the dark no matter what. I preferred a few minutes of rest to prepare for what I suspected would be a long night.

Determination set in. This would not be my last swim.

After 15 minutes, I flipped back to my stomach, dropped my face into the water, and began kicking again.

The depth of the water had changed. The shallowing slope was too gradual to notice. But now the sandy bottom lay only about 20 feet deep. Still deep enough to drown me, but it encouraged me to know I was closer to solid ground.

Two more hours passed. The sun had vanished, and the stars were the only thing visible. Every few minutes, I paused long enough to take a bearing off the stars. I understand the concepts behind celestial navigation, and if I was on *Carina*, I could use a sextant and a guide book to get a heading. Here, my only goal was to keep going north. The North Star was ideal for that.

I said a brief prayer, thanking God that it wasn't overcast.

In the distance, I noticed a light–a passing boat, at least three miles away. Even if it came this way, I would never be visible in the night. During the day, it would be difficult to make out my bobbing in the waves. At night, the task was impossible.

I wondered how the bull shark was doing? As ominous as his presence was, at least he was company. The utter voidness that permeated everything out here grew unsettling. At least the times I'd been out on the ocean in the dark before, I always had the comfort of *Carina's* deck. The VHF radio would squawk occasionally. The chart plotter would beep.

Now, I had the splashing of waves. Incessant splashing.

I straightened my body and rolled up to rest for a few minutes. The running lights in the distance seemed to be closer. I hoped they were on a heading for me.

After my brain counted out ten minutes, I decided I had rested long enough. Once I located my heading with the North Star, I started swimming again.

The next few hours were a steady drive. My mind now had an in-depth conversation with my stomach. The discussion concerned how far the nearest conch stand would be when I reached shore. Fried conch fritters and a conch sandwich would hit the spot. I could down two or three Sands beers too. After a gallon of water.

The constant drumming in my head had continued for hours. It had remained the same consistency, and while I was ready for it to stop, I couldn't slow down to worry about it.

My muscles ached too, and I wanted to chalk that up to 14 hours of swimming. If I'd been getting a mile an hour, then I should be about halfway there. If. If. If.

Four more hours passed, and everything started to hurt. I'd shot past just regular pain. Everything burned; my eyes felt dry, and I had to stop far more frequently. The temperature of the water had turned so cold overnight. During the day, the sun offset it, and now I shivered as my pace slowed.

An hour ago, I noticed a few lights ahead, and I kept moving toward them. They were white, not the standard red and green of running lights. That meant anchor lights or, better yet, shore. I had plenty of time to speculate. I guessed they were at least five or six miles away.

The night sky faded as dawn approached. The snorkel made it easier for me to avoid straining my neck for air, and I kept my head down as I swam along. Only lifting it every few minutes to ensure I hadn't veered off-course. I wondered how the Olympic swimmers learned to swim a straight line. Of course, I reminded myself, that they only had to cover the distance of an Olympic-sized pool.

The graying morning brought life back to the void I'd been trapped in. As light spread across the sea, I paused for rest. A splash jerked my attention to the west, where a dolphin surfaced a few hundred feet away.

I heaved a sigh of relief when I saw the outline of an island ahead. The lights I had seen had come from there. I still needed to swim a few miles, but a renewed vigor washed over me. My feet pushed me forward.

Another hour passed as the sun rose. Almost as soon as it crested the horizon, I could feel its warmth on my back.

An outboard motor broke through the din of water splashing around me. Stopping, I used the fins to push me up out of the water for a look around. A quarter of a mile away, I spotted a small fishing boat.

My fins lifted me up again, and I waved my arms frantically as the boat motored my direction. Each time I sank down, I mustered my strength and rose again, with my arms flailing about.

Two men were in the boat, and the one in the front pointed my direction after the sixth time I came out of the water.

Jumping out again, I shouted, "Here! Over here!"

The boat veered and began a direct path to me. As I sank down in the water, I exhaled in relief.

"Are you alright?" the man in the bow asked as his partner nudged alongside me.

Shaking my head, I gasped, "No, I need help."

The two men appeared to be in their 60s and judging from the accent, they were locals. They both hooked their hands under my arms and dragged me over the gunwale. After rolling onto the floor, I thanked them.

"I've been in the water since yesterday," I explained, pulling the mask and snorkel off my head.

The man in the bow reached into a bag and pulled out a bottle of water.

"Thank you," I mumbled as I pulled the cap off and turned the bottle up.

"We don't have any food," he told me.

"Water's good," I breathed out between swallows.

The driver pushed the tiller on the outboard to one side and turned the tiny wooden boat back toward land.

"Is this Andros?" I asked after draining the water bottle.

"Yeah," he answered me.

I attempted to push up onto the seat, but collapsed as my legs gave out. Finally, my arm caught the gunwale, and I pulled myself into a seated position on the bottom of the boat.

The man in the bow stared at me with piqued curiosity.

29

The little Toyota sat on the road in front of the house. I was waiting for Richman to come home, and it had been close to three hours since I parked here. The engine had been off, and in the hot Key sun, the inside was a sweltering oven. My skin was clammy and wet, and I was working on my sixth bottle of water.

Alexander and David fished me out of the water two days ago. After I interrupted their morning fishing trip, they were kind enough to bring me back to their tiny village. The local doctor deemed me healthy enough. He prescribed a lot of water and rest but thought that if I had any adverse reaction to cutting short my decompression, it must have been minor. Nevertheless, he recommended a visit to my own doctor when I was Stateside.

Unfortunately, I didn't have time for that. I was going to take the Bahamian doctor's word for it. If I was going to find Wexler, there was no time for doctors.

With little to offer the two fishermen, I traded my fins and snorkel gear for a ride to a larger town, where some

American cruisers often anchored. After a few phone calls, I found a friend of a friend that brought me back to South Florida.

A little ingenuity and an ability to hot-wire a car got me from Miami to the Keys without drawing any attention. All that trouble to get here, and Richman wasn't around. Pretty damned inconsiderate of him.

A BMW pulled past me, and I watched as the silver car pulled into Richman's driveway. He was the only one in the vehicle, which was a good sign. For me, not for him. If there were any witnesses around for the next hour, it would create a score of problems.

Five minutes passed, and I removed the Glock 9 mm from the glove compartment. Wiping down the inside of the car, I wanted to make sure that I left no fingerprints behind. The Toyota Corolla had been "borrowed" from a hotel near Islamorada. The gun was one I kept hidden on *Carina*. It had no ties to me, and I didn't declare it when I crossed to the Caribbean. It was a little piece of insurance that I could drop over the side of the boat if need be.

If the next few minutes went according to my plan, I would not be using this car again.

I rang the doorbell and waited. Finally, the door opened, and Paul Richman stared at me.

"What are you doing here?" he gasped.

My palm caught him on the chest and shoved him inside. The lawyer landed on his ass. As I slammed the door behind me, I stepped onto the marbled foyer floor.

"Who the hell do you think you are?" he demanded, trying to stand up.

The 9 mm snapped up from behind my back. The barrel pressed against his forehead.

"Uh..." he stammered.

"I'm going to ask you a few questions."

"What do you want?"

My glare silenced him.

"You're going to tell me everything I want to know," I explained in a monotone voice.

"I don't know anything," he blabbered.

My forearm cocked back, and the top of the Glock slammed into his temple. The lawyer tumbled into a glass table, sending it crashing to the floor and spilling a vase of fresh tulips. As he stared up at me, he swallowed hard as the barrel returned to his forehead.

"Don't bullshit me," I scolded. "At least have the decency to wait until I ask a question to lie to me."

"I wasn't lying," he muttered.

My head tilted to about a 45-degree angle. I considered hitting him again.

"Maybe you should only talk when I ask you a question."

He nodded.

"Where is Daniel Wexler?"

"Who?"

The next blow shattered his cheekbone. The crunch was audible as the bottom of the pistol slammed into his face. Richman teetered on his knees. His hands clutched his face.

"I don't mind beating you to death," I warned him. "I'll drag your body off the cliff out there and let the crabs feast on you."

He quivered. Every movement caused his broken face to wince. Each flinch caused more pain. I dialed my empathy back when I considered what might have happened to Rikki.

"Now," I spoke with deliberation, "tell me where Daniel Wexler is."

"I'm not sure," he announced, raising his hands to block whatever I might throw at him.

"Let's speculate," I ordered. "When did you last talk to him?"

"Three days ago."

"What about?"

He stared at me. His eyes shifting between my face and the barrel of the Glock. He didn't want to tell me. Not because he was hiding it. He was scared of what my reaction might be.

"Better to tell me," I pointed out, "than for me to drag it out of you."

"He told me that he had the gold."

"And?" I prodded.

"He said you were dead."

I cleared my throat. "Well, this is awkward, isn't it?"

"I didn't know…"

"What?" I asked. "You didn't know that I wasn't dead? Or you didn't know that he was going to kill me?"

"Yes, that," he assured me. "I had no idea he was going to kill you."

"Do you actually care for me that much?"

"I didn't want any trouble," he vowed.

"What about the day that we came to see you?" I asked him. "Did you want any trouble that day?"

He shook his head, wincing from the pain.

"But you called those friends of yours."

"No, I promise. I called Daniel. He said that he would take care of it."

As I shifted the gun to my other hand, I leaned toward his face. "Take care of it?"

His head moved in a slow nod.

"Take care of it," I repeated. "That sounds ominous. You didn't think it sounded like a threat?"

He blinked at me, shaking his head so that the movement caused less pain.

"I think you're bullshitting me."

"I didn't know," he pleaded fervently.

"Did he tell you about the girl?"

Nodding, he responded, "Yes, he said she was still alive."

"What does he plan to do with her?"

"He didn't tell me. I honestly don't know. He said he's taking her to Valhalla."

"Valhalla?" I questioned. "The Norse heaven?"

"No," he explained. "Valhalla is what we call the island. It's going to be a sovereign state."

"What?" I stared at him, completely dumbfounded.

"Daniel is building an island where he can start his own government. Only certain people will be allowed in. It will be a sanctuary."

"A sanctuary," I repeated. "For whites?"

Richman nodded. "Daniel said it will be for God's ultimate people. His chosen race."

"You guys don't read a lot about God, do you?"

He stared at me.

"The gold?" I asked, ignoring the irony. "Is that why he wants it?"

"He figures it was our birthright. Since the Fatherland fell, it should belong to those of us trying to revive it."

"And you told him about it? Since Henry was your grandfather."

"He's both of our grandfather. Daniel is my cousin."

While relaxing my grip on the gun, I let him talk. He was on auto-pilot, and the threat of death still loomed around me.

"Our grandfather hated his background. We grew up hearing the stories of what happened that night. His plan was to run away when they landed in Nassau, but the boat never docked there. When he couldn't get away at Baxter's, he thought he was trapped. When the explosion happened, he realized he had his chance."

"His name was Heinrich Vogel. He worked in the radio room. As the crew tried to save the ship, he made his way to the gold and escaped through one of the hatches. He survived for days on the little inflatable life raft. Until a storm capsized it. The fisherman that saved him had no idea who or what he was."

"After your grandfather went through all that to get away, you want to recreate it?"

Richman huffed. "Our grandfather was a traitor and a coward."

"And you and your cousin feel like, somehow, the Nazis got it right?"

"You wouldn't understand," he mumbled.

"Oh, I get it. You don't like how unfair life is for all the whites. I mean, here you are, living on the ocean in one of the most expensive and, dare I say, white areas of the United States. You have a $100,000 car, two planes, and who-knows what else, but life's unfair."

"I earned all that," he insisted. "I didn't get it because I was a different color."

"Bullshit!" I howled. "You got it because your grandfather made off with the Führer's gold."

"That's not the only reason."

"Shut up before I hit you again," I warned him. "Your grandfather braved the open ocean to escape that life. That's not cowardice."

He started to retort, and I glared at him. His mouth clamped shut.

While I stared at him, I felt my face contort. His behavior was incredulous. How can anyone have these kinds of thoughts? How do you throw about the name of God in your argument? The man drew bile into my mouth.

"Where is your Valhalla?"

"It's south of Cuba. He arranged with the Cuban government to have a piece of their water. He's building there now."

"Building?" I inquired. "How?"

"Daniel and I acquired two retired aircraft carriers from Venezuela. Another one from Malaysia is coming. They are being moored together. When it's all finished, we will house 2,000 people of our choosing."

"I'm guessing this kind of white utopia won't be cheap, right?"

Richman stared at me.

"Let me rephrase that," I said. "What's the going rate to move away from all the brown people?"

"Three million."

"Exclusivity ain't cheap," I retorted. "I'll stick with my soul, though."

He exhaled a scoffing breath.

"How do we get to your little paradise?"

His eyes cut toward the window as he bit his lip. After picking a spot I was sure would do minimal damage, I fired a round into his shoulder, knocking him back against the wall.

He bellowed in pain. I dug the barrel of the Glock into the fresh wound, and he cried out, tears streaming down his face.

"Let me explain," I growled through gritted teeth. "The only way you survive today is if you take me there."

"I can fly there," he whimpered.

"I thought you could," I responded, gripping his injured arm and dragging him to his feet. "Let's go."

Richman shuffled his feet as we climbed down the iron steps that were bolted to the face of the cliff. The de Havilland was tied up on the dock below.

"He's going to kill you," Richman offered. "He has a small army."

"So far," I contradicted, as I prodded him in the back, "his small army has done nothing but piss me off. Besides, I don't plan to tell him I'm coming."

We reached the bottom of the steps, and Richman slowed his pace. He was glancing around, trying to weigh his chances.

"I don't think I can fly like this," he moaned.

"Can you swim like that?"

He turned and stared at me with a shocked look.

I continued, "Didn't think so. Get your ass in the plane."

30

The trip south took four hours. Once we were in the air, I forced Paul Richman into the back, where I secured him. He pinpointed on the map the location of Valhalla. Richman didn't strike me as the bold type. He wasn't about to die for his own cause. However, I didn't trust that some brief moment of resolve might prompt him to drive the plane into the ocean. Better for me if he was out of the way for the time being.

"Tell me about the island," I ordered.

"What do you want to know?"

"Does it have any defenses?"

"Yes," the man answered. "There are two anti-aircraft guns mounted on either end of the islands."

"What kind of rounds?"

"I'm... not sure."

"What's Wexler going to do when you show up unannounced?" I asked Richman.

"I don't know," he stammered.

"Let's hope he doesn't shoot us down," I commented.

"He knows my plane," he said, hoping that I might be deterred.

It had been 15 years or more since I'd been holding the stick in an airplane. The de Havilland wasn't too fancy. Richman had attempted to maintain the vintage instrumentation and controls, which worked well for me. My experience was on single-engine sod-hoppers. The concept wasn't challenging once the plane was airborne. A successful landing, on the other hand, might be another story.

The first pass I made gave me an excellent view of Wexler's Valhalla. It was two aircraft carriers attached to each other. They weren't as big as the one's the U.S. Navy deployed, but they offered a large surface area. The runways were being converted into greenery. Dirt and grass covered large sections, and small trees and gardens were already growing in those areas. Buildings were being constructed along the edges of these greened areas.

Talitha was tied up along a dock constructed on the southern side of the "island." There didn't seem to be any movement on deck, and I allowed myself to worry about Rikki for a minute.

The radio chirped, and a voice erupted from the speaker. "Unidentified aircraft come in. You are entering the airspace of the sovereign nation of Valhalla."

With a look over my shoulder at Richman, I sighed. "Seriously, Valhalla was the best you guys could come up with? That doesn't bode well for your movement."

He didn't answer.

"I repeat, you are entering the airspace..."

I cut the speaker off. "Get up here and request clearance," I ordered Richman. "If you do anything stupid, I'll toss you out the door."

He nodded and squirmed forward. He took too long with his hands and feet bound, but I didn't plan on cutting him loose.

With the microphone held to his mouth, Richman responded, "de Havilland niner oh one Charlie Papa requesting permission to land."

There was some silence on the other end. After several seconds, a deep voice responded, "de Havilland niner oh one Charlie Papa, permission granted. Paullie is that you?"

"Affirmative, Daniel."

"Is there a problem?" Wexler's voice asked over the radio.

My eyes cut toward Richman, who locked eyes with me and blinked. "I'll tell you about it when I land."

"Affirmative, Paul. Come up to command."

"Roger," Richman responded.

"That better not have been some sly message between you two," I warned.

He shook his head. "No, but he is going to wonder why I'm showing up unannounced."

"What is command?"

"Daniel's idea of a central command for the island. It's the bridge on the northern carrier. He can see all the cameras from there."

"Where would they keep Rikki?" I asked.

"She might be in the brig," he offered, "but I don't know."

Once I lined up alongside the dock, I adjusted the flaps and pushed the yoke down.

"You do know how to land?" Richman asked from behind me.

"I got the principles down," I promised him.

"I'm not buckled in," he told me.

"That's a risk I'm willing to take," I said off-handedly.

As I released the throttle while we were descending, I worried I was coming in too fast.

Richman confirmed that, saying, "You're going too fast!"

I could hear him scrambling around in the back, trying to find a secure place in case we crashed. The pontoons hit the water and bounced over a six-foot wave. I tried to slow the propeller as we leaped over a wave again. The flaps were peeled back on the wings as I slowed faster. Each subsequent bounce was smaller until we were rocking over the waves like a top heavy canoe.

"Like riding a bike," I assured Richman, who let out a string of expletives.

"Paul," I reminded him, "you've been doing good, but the only way you survive today is if you stay right where you are. Don't try to warn Wexler or his men. Do you understand?"

"Yeah," he muttered.

With the butt of the Glock, I smashed the radio in the cockpit. He might have been a man of his word, but I wanted to ensure his cooperation.

Guiding the de Havilland through the rough waters was tricky. There was no hull to ride through the waves. Instead, the pontoons were pitching the entire plane from side to side. Finally, after two passes, I stopped right alongside the dock. Two men stood there with dock lines, waiting to secure the plane.

As they tied off the cleats, I moved around to the door, gave Richman a warning stare, and opened the latch. The closest of the two men extended a hand to help me out of the plane. If he knew who Richman was, he didn't seem to realize I wasn't him. Often the mind plays wicked tricks on us. This might have been one of those times for this guy.

As I stepped out of the plane, the Glock slid up against his chest and I pulled the trigger. The muffled gunshot was lost to the sea, but the other dockhand jerked his head toward me at the same moment his partner fell into the water. The next shot hit the second man in the face. He fell to the deck, and I pushed his body into the sea with his friend.

The plastic deck pitched in the rough water. A metal-rung ladder stretched up to the next level. With the Glock nestled in my waistband, I climbed. The ladder stopped on a platform that inclined toward the top level.

Just short of the top, I peered over the edge. There were six men in my line of sight. Three cameras were hanging on posts around the area.

From my point, I could make out both superstructures for the respective carriers.

Act like you belong. When my buddy Jay and I were on leave in London, we crashed the wedding of some movie star. He brought me a tuxedo and told me those four words, "Act like you belong." We made it through the door, and Jay ended up in the hotel room of some cut-rate actress.

I wasn't tuxedoed up, but I could pretend. My shirt covered the Glock, and my head stayed level. Two of the men on deck were armed with the same model H&K that Bushy Beard had. The other four were workers. They appeared to be putting together a prefab building. If I planned to head toward the superstructure where I suspected the command center would be, I needed to steer clear of the two gunmen. The longer I could stay incognito, the more chance of success I might have.

That lasted about 15 seconds. One man touched his ear, a terrible habit when wearing a radio. It's the automatic signal to anyone around that you just got a message. My gut told me the message was about me.

"Grab him!" the first one shouted across the deck to the second guard.

My hand snapped up with the Glock and fired three rounds, catching the first guy center mass. Turning, I dropped to one knee and fired two more into the second guard before he could get the muzzle of his H&K up. The four workers scrambled away from the gunfire.

Once I jumped to my feet, I sprinted toward the second gunman and scooped up his H&K. Ahead, shouting erupted as three men poured out of the door at the bottom of the superstructure. Squeezing the trigger, I sprayed bullets in their direction. The first two that came out the door jerked as the rounds tore through their bodies. The third jumped back through the doorway as the others fell to the ground.

As I charged toward the door, I fired several rounds into the steel door. There wasn't much chance that they penetrated the metal, but I was betting they sent the gunman running from the door. My shoulder slammed the door open, and he fired into the metal from the other side. My hand raised the H&K along the edge of the door and squeezed the trigger. The gun vibrated my arm as a burst of bullets fired into the narrow stairwell. With a thud, the weight of the man fell against the door, and I stepped back to let him slide to the floor.

I dropped the empty gun, picked up the stairwell guy's weapon, and began climbing the stairs. This wasn't going quite like I had hoped, which was par for the course when I rely on brute force. I needed to find Rikki. Wexler could keep the gold. At least for now. As long as I found her safe.

The door at the top of the stairs opened a few inches, and I caught the hand on the knob and jerked him down the steps. A smaller man tumbled past me, and I turned and planted a foot against him to shove him the rest of the way. The door swung open, and I took a quick look through the passageway. The hallway was clear.

With the MP7 pointed at the man at the bottom of the stairs, I hurried down to his level.

"Where's the girl?" I hissed.

His eyes widened. The gunman wasn't much more than a kid, maybe 25 or 26 years old. He signed on for the white rage and never expected a full-contact battle.

"Daniel's got her locked in his quarters."

"Where are they?" I demanded.

He shook his head. "He has it guarded."

The muzzle of the gun pressed against his face. "Does it look like I care?"

"I don't wanna die," he pleaded.

"Here's the thing, kid," I explained in a monotone voice. "You joined up with an army of racist idiots. You are carrying around machine guns and playing the part. You signed up for it."

"Please," he begged, tears welling up in his eyes. "I want to go home."

"Take me to the girl," I ordered.

A quick nod, and I pulled him to his feet.

"It's up there." He pointed up the stairs.

While marching behind him, I held the barrel of the H&K just over his shoulder.

"They might be waiting for you," he informed me.

"You better hope they like you enough to hold their fire."

"Shit," he mumbled. "Please, sir."

"Open the damned door," I commanded.

He pulled the door open. The hallway was still empty. If Wexler had any forces in this section, I would have expected them to converge.

Keep an eye on your six, Gordon.

"Keep moving," I insisted.

The corridor had three doors, two on the forward side and one aft. Thus, there were two levels above us, and the bridge would be on the top level. Wexler, with his superiority complex, had no doubt taken the Captain's Quarters, which were generally located just off the bridge.

"That door takes you up," he told me, pointing at the aft door.

"Lead the way," I said.

"They'll kill me."

As I was about to explain to the kid that not obeying me might result in the same thing, footsteps echoed up the staircase we just exited. Twisting, I let loose a burst of bullets as the door swung open. The bullets riddled the walls along the hallway, and I let go of the kid and dropped to the ground, firing through the door.

31

Without a backward glance, the kid took off in the commotion. With a bang, the door behind me slammed shut as he rabbited away. The first man through the stairwell door caught the first round. A second attempted to crawl over him, but I shot him twice in the head.

No time to waste. I scampered to my feet. As I jerked open the door to the bridge, I raised the H&K up the stairwell. It was empty. After charging up the steps, I stopped at the top stair. I grabbed the handle and swung it open. A burst of gunfire peppered the door, and I pulled back.

After dropping down two steps, I extended the barrel past the door frame, just inches above the deck, and fired. As the gunfire strafed the hallway, I heard the howls as my bullets chewed through the legs of a couple of men. A quick peek found two men floundering on the floor, unable to stand on their shredded calves.

The H&K in my hands was low on ammo, and I unloaded the rest into the injured men. I tossed the empty gun and picked up both of their weapons. Three doors were on this hallway, too. One at the end with a sign in Spanish that I guessed read "Bridge" or whatever the Spanish equivalent was. The one on the starboard side read "Capitán."

My hand touched the handle. The knob rotated until I felt the click, and I pushed it open.

Rikki stared at me from the bed. Her eyes met mine, and she jumped up and ran to me.

"I thought you were dead!" she bellowed.

"Not yet," I admitted. "But the day is young."

She kissed me and wrapped her arms around me.

"Did they hurt you?"

She shook her head. "As soon as he realized who my father was, Wexler saw a payday. He warned his people to leave me alone in case he needed 'proof of life.'"

The door I had come from opened and two men barreled through the entryway. My right hand came up and sprayed them with bullets as I pushed Rikki into the quarters.

"We need to move," I told her, handing her one of the H&K's in my hand. "Shoot at anything that moves, as long as it's not me."

"How did you get here?" she asked.

"I brought Richman's plane," I explained. "But we won't be able to get out of here that way."

"Why not?"

"Wexler's got anti-aircraft guns. So we'd never be able to take off without him shooting us down."

"They brought me in *Talitha*," she suggested.

"She's not fast enough," I informed her. "They'd be able to sink her down before we could get very far."

"Damn them," she grunted, adding, "They have a submarine."

Turning, I looked at her–that made sense. We never saw them coming. Not on the island or at the wreck site. Because they were underwater.

"Do you know where it is?" I asked.

She shook her head.

"How do you feel about storming the bridge?"

"Can we kill that bastard?"

While peering around the door frame, I responded, "I have every intention of doing just that."

With a motion for her to follow me, I moved toward the bridge. No one else had come through the door, and I expected there to be at least a few men up there with Wexler.

When the door opened, the metal stairs reverberated with three gunshots. They were shooting semi-automatics. I considered that to be on the bright side. If we charged up the stairs, we were in a shooting gallery. That was the downside.

Each of us clung to the wall on either side of the door. Waiting on something.

"What do we do?" Rikki asked.

My H&K fired up the stairs. There was no aiming, just me squeezing the trigger. Two gunshots retorted back, striking the floor at the bottom of the stairs.

My eyes scanned the hallway. We would have reinforcements coming up behind us soon.

"The fire extinguisher," I nodded to the red cylinder hanging on the wall. Next to it was a reel of fire hose. Fire is the last thing anyone wants on any ship, and they have so many redundant systems to squash any flames before they spread. They might work for us.

Rikki grabbed the extinguisher and tossed it across the opening. The boys up top were trigger happy and fired two rounds as the red tank passed the door.

"Cover fire," I ordered Rikki, who stuck her gun around the corner and squeezed off eight rounds in half a second.

It was long enough for me to place the bottom of the cylinder on the second step and let the handle rest on the floor. With a swift motion, I pulled my Glock from my waistband and fired one round into the metal top.

The bullet ripped the top off and the compressed air turned the extinguisher into a red rocket that blasted up the stairs, leaving a thick fog of chemicals in its wake. Two shots erupted, followed by some unintelligible shouting. My knees bent, dropping me into a crouch as I charged up the stairs through the fog.

The first bullet grazed my shoulder, and I fired a spray of shots through the cloud and dropped to my stomach on the stairs. Four rounds went over my head, and I returned fire. A body collapsed and rolled down the stairs until it hit me.

"Cover!" I shouted to Rikki.

Thinking short thoughts, I tried to get lower than the steps as she fired five shots over me.

"Stop!" I yelled, and I grabbed the body a few steps above me and pulled it toward me.

He wasn't a big fellow, which would have its advantage and disadvantages. He was light enough for me to hoist up as a shield. Hopefully, he wasn't so skinny that he couldn't provide the cover I needed. With the corpse covering my chest, I crawled up the steps, firing through the fog.

Once I lifted him up, I fired six rounds toward the top of the stairs. A thud sounded as another body dropped. The cloud of chemicals was dissipating, but I couldn't make out if there was anyone else. Despite that, I wasn't going to waste what cover I had left. Using the body as a shield, I worked my way up the steps.

The body in my arms jerked as a bullet hit him, and I squeezed the trigger, aiming toward the sound. The gun ran dry, but a figure slumped forward through the haze and fell toward me.

Too many bodies to deal with. I dropped my shield and my empty H&K before coming up with my Glock. The last few stairs opened up onto the bridge. Two men crouched with guns drawn. I pulled back against the wall as they both fired.

From my position, I could see the windows that overlooked the runways. The reflection in the glass gave me a clear view of the two men waiting on me to step back through the doorway. Behind them, I could make out the image of Daniel Wexler.

"Chase!" Rikki shouted from below. "I got company."

Gunfire erupted below as she laid down a round of suppressive fire. She clamored up the steps until she was just beneath me.

"There are three of them," she informed me.

"Hold them there," I ordered.

She grunted something and sprayed three rounds at the foot of the stairs.

"Wexler!" I shouted.

"Gordon," he responded, "you must be a helluva swimmer."

"What do you think is going to happen here?" I asked.

"I figure you'll try to kill me, and my boys here will drop you first."

"It's not working out for your boys so far, Daniel."

Wexler chuckled, "You're a little pinned down right now."

With a deep breath, I twisted, fired, and pulled back as both of the two crouching fired simultaneously. When the ringing from the gunshots subsided, I studied the reflection. Only one man remained at the ready. The other had fallen out of view.

"Other guy," I spoke loudly. "Just so you know what you are going against. I was trained by the United States Marine Corps for exactly this kind of operation. As you can see, I am much more accurate than you are. So, while the next round you shoot might hit me, I promise the next one I shoot will get you."

"Don't listen to him," Wexler blustered.

Rikki fired three more shots at the door below.

"I'm running low, Chase," she whispered.

"Grab one of these guy's guns. We're almost done here."

She let out a sigh. "I hope that's the good-kind of 'done.'"

"Fellow." I started talking again. "This is your last chance. Ditch Wexler, and you get to walk out of here."

The man in the reflection glanced back at Wexler, and while I couldn't make out his face, I knew he was weighing his options. Finally, he dropped the gun onto the deck.

Wexler moved to grab the weapon, and I swung around the wall with my Glock leveled at him.

"Don't," I demanded.

He froze, half-way bent toward the gun. Sneering, he straightened up and stared at me.

"What now, Gordon?"

As I looked at the man, kneeling on the floor with his hands behind his head, I asked, "What's your name?"

"Jason McCormick," he responded.

He was in his mid-20s, and there was some spark I recognized in him. "Military or police?" I asked.

"What?" he stammered.

"Jason, shut up," Wexler ordered.

Squeezing the trigger, I blew out Wexler's right knee, sending him to the ground in a clump. "Don't talk, Daniel, until I'm ready for you."

He groaned in pain.

As my attention turned back to Jason, I repeated. "Military or police? Which one did you get fired from?"

His eyes shifted down. "Army."

"Makes sense," I snarled. "Might be time to reevaluate your morals, kid."

He glanced up at me. Despite the fear, there was still a ton of hatred in his eyes, and I knew that the world would likely be a better place if I put him down now. He wasn't going to change. This experience was only going to bolster his belief that he was being slighted somehow because of his race. He'd never see himself as the loser he was.

Today, though, wasn't my day to dispose of him.

"My suggestion to you," I said, "is to get your ass off this boat. Once I'm done with Wexler, I'm cleaning house."

He nodded curtly and rose to his feet.

"Run along, kid. Tell your friends."

He wasted no time running for the stairwell. He couldn't resist glaring at Rikki as he slid past her and fled down the stairs. Three gunshots sounded from below, and I imagined Jason didn't make it past his comrades.

"Get up," I ordered Wexler.

"I can't," he argued. "My leg."

With the pressure of the muzzle against his temple, I silently encouraged him to obey me. He pushed up onto his good knee. The other leg hung limply behind him as he pulled himself up.

"What now?" he muttered.

"The gold? Where is it?"

"Locked up in the vault," he chuckled through a groan. "You'll need me to open it, asshole. Guess what, ain't gonna happen."

"That makes you utterly useless to me," I pointed out.

"You'll never make it out of here," he whimpered.

"If you don't want to help me, you'll die right here."

"Rikki," I called to her. "How do you feel about letting bygones be bygones?"

"As long as we leave with the gold, I don't give a flying shit about that racist bastard."

"There ya go," I told Wexler. "Your one and only 'get out of jail free' card. Want to use it?"

As he stared up into my eyes, he considered his chances. Was I truthful? Was he willing to die for his beliefs? Finally, he nodded.

She stood vigilantly at the top of the stairs. Turning toward me, she lifted an eyebrow in response.

"Step back," I advised her.

She obeyed, and I hooked Wexler under the arm and thrust him toward the stairs. He hobbled and stumbled forward, but I jerked him up by his collar.

"What are you doing?"

"I still don't trust you, so you're going first."

"Boys," I shouted down the steps, "the boss is on his way down!"

"Hope they don't shoot you too," I whispered in his ear a second before I shoved him down the metal stairs. Wexler tumbled down the steps, crying in agony.

"Shit," Rikki huffed in surprise.

As I smiled back at her, I pointed at the weapons on the ground and told her, "Grab those guns."

Without waiting for her, I followed Wexler down. He lay at the bottom, still breathing.

"Good," I stated, "You're still alive."

After dragging him back up on his one foot, I pushed him through the bottom door. Jason's body was still bleeding next to the other guard I killed earlier. Two men stared at me from a few feet away. They each had a .45 leveled at us and matching H&K MP7s.

"Daniel," I questioned, "what did you do? Was there a sale at the Heckler & Koch store?"

The two men were closer in age to the men who chased us onto Pine Key. Both had the look of hardened men, complete with neck tattoos.

"Don't shoot," Wexler pleaded through a bloodied face.

"I think your men are confused," I commented. "Tell them to put down the guns."

"Not gonna happen," the one on the right rasped.

Rikki's footsteps were coming down the stairs behind me. I kept my eyes on both men. The .45s could tear through Wexler and do a fair bit of damage to me. As long as they didn't want to shoot their leader, we were in a stand-off. I could drop one with ease, but the other would have time to fire.

"Screw it," I hissed, firing a round into the right's chest, and turning Wexler toward the other.

His gun flared, and the shot echoed through the hall. Pulling the trigger, I caught him in the throat with the bullet. Wexler's body became dead weight as his man's bullet tore into his chest.

As his body collapsed, I checked both men to ensure they were dead. As I looked back at Wexler, I watched as his heart pumped a fountain of blood from his chest for a few more seconds before the light went out in his eyes.

32

"The gold?"

We stood in the hallway with bodies littered around us. The only person who could take us to the gold had bled out on the floor.

"I think we have to cut our losses," I commented.

"Ugh!" she grunted.

"Chaos is about to ensue here, and my guess is that the Cuban military will swarm this little utopia pretty soon."

"Cuba?" she questioned.

"Yeah," I explained, "Wexler is building this little island on the edge of Cuban waters."

She snorted in laughter. My head turned to study her. "What?" I asked.

"The Cubans will end up with the gold."

With a smirk across my face, I quipped, "Better late than never."

"How many of his people are left?"

I shook my head, admitting, "I'm not sure. More than we want to face."

Rikki walked over to the wall where the fire extinguisher had been hanging. The emergency alarm switch was mounted next to the empty extinguisher case. Pulling down on the lever, she started the screaming sound of the warning alarm throughout the ship.

My hand grabbed hers as I dragged her back down the next flight of stairs. We spilled out the door to see men running around in a clamor. Now was the time to make our escape.

We started running across the former tarmac for the dock where *Talitha* was tied. I heard the familiar chunking sound and skidded to a stop. Fifty feet from us, Bushy Beard was moving toward us. The barrel of a 12-gauge shotgun rested in the palm of his left hand. His right hand gripped the pistol grip.

"Thought I left you with the sharks," he grunted.

My Glock snapped up, and I put the sights on his chest. "Yeah, he was great fun."

"Wexler?" Bushy Beard asked.

"Dead."

The biker shook his head in dismay. He paced back and forth in a semi-circle that reminded me of the bull shark. "Guess it's going to be a free-for-all here," he commented, considering the ramifications of a power shift.

"That does seem to be a possibility," I answered.

"You're going for the gold, I assume?" he asked.

Rikki stirred next to me, shifting her weight from one leg to the other.

"Just planning to leave," I told him.

A quick motion caught my eye, as Rikki jerked the .45 in her hand up and fired four shots into Bushy Beard. He stumbled back and tried to bring the shotgun level with us. I fired two more shots that sprawled him on his back.

"He was an asshole," she stated in defense.

"No argument there," I agreed.

We reached the ramp to the dock, and I saw three men trying to untie *Talitha*. Everyone could tell a sinking ship when they saw one, and any ride off was fair game. I fired at a man trying to free the stern line. The bullets hit the dock in front of him. My aim was intentional. I was getting a little sick of the killing, and a warning shot at an unarmed combatant seemed justified.

The result was a frightened man that fell off the dock into the water. Rikki didn't offer a warning, firing a round into the man at the bow. Her bullet knocked him to the deck, but the wound looked superficial.

I grabbed the steel ladder and slid down it. Rikki followed me at a slower pace. The third man was standing on the flybridge, ready to pull away once his buddies finished untying the yacht. Instead, he pulled a pistol and fired at us.

My return fire sent him cowering for cover, and I jumped over the aft rail to board the boat. As I burst through the sliding glass doors, I found Paul Richman standing at the stairs leading to the next deck. He fired a gun at me, and the bullet shattered the glass of the door. The Glock in my hand popped up and fired. My shot hit him in the shoulder, twisting him around. A second round caught him in the back.

As I climbed over him, I kicked the 9 mm he fired at me away from him. He was still breathing, but he wasn't going anywhere.

"I told you to stay on the plane if you wanted to survive."

The lawyer wheezed a response that I didn't care about.

Behind the captain's chair, another kid shook in fear. He was about the same age as Jason with the same social reject vibe to him. The kind of wasted youth that someone like Daniel Wexler can convince to join his cause. The .45 in his hand was rocking, and he was too scared to either drop it or point it at me.

With the Glock leveled at the kid, I told him. "One chance. Get off this ship before I count to three."

The .45 clattered to the ground as the kid rose to his feet and ran for the rail. He launched himself over the side and splashed into the sea below.

As I glanced over the edge, I found Rikki still on the dock.

"Untie us," I called to her.

The kid had already started the engines. The only thing left to do was get off the dock.

"Clear!" I heard Rikki shout, and I pushed the throttles forward.

The engines rumbled as the big yacht motored off the dock. The gas gauges showed that both fuel tanks were over half-full. Enough that I opened the throttles all the way. The more distance I could put between us and Wexler's Valhalla, the better I would feel.

"Richman?" she asked.

"Yeah," I confirmed. "He must have gotten himself free. He should have stayed on the plane."

She wrapped her arms around me, and my hand touched her arm. She breathed out.

"I thought you were dead," she admitted after a minute.

As I squeezed her forearm, I agreed, "I thought you might be too."

"He wasn't going to let me go, even if Dad paid his ransom. He planned to take *Talitha* out and sink her with me on her. So they kept me tied up in the engine room for days. Until we got there yesterday."

I started to tell her how lucky she was, but I sensed maybe it wasn't true. She tightened her grip on me.

"What do we do now?" she asked.

Turning to look up at her, I suggested, "We have a long ride back to the Keys."

"Good," she sighed, "I don't think I can handle any more people for a while."

"We could take a little sabbatical," I offered. "Jamaica is only 100 miles southwest of here. We could find a nice quiet anchorage, where we could hide until we are ready to see the real world."

She smiled and kissed my cheek. "I could handle that."

"You need some rest," I told her. "I'm going to take care of Paul. Why don't you go clean up?"

With the autopilot set to take us toward the northern coast of Jamaica, I climbed down stairs. Richman was no longer breathing, which was a relief because alive or dead I was going to drag him out and toss him off the aft deck.

The lawyer bounced off the swim platform before being swallowed by the yacht's wake.

While Rikki was resting, I called Milo Oder from the satellite phone on the bridge.

"Milo," I began, "Let me start by saying that this conversation isn't taking place."

"Son, I'm not even at home," he replied.

"Are you acquainted with anyone that might be interested in a couple of aircraft carriers floating in the Cuban waters?"

"I know lots of people interested in lots of things," he remarked.

"Let's say that it's not much more than a floating heap of human garbage, but someone should do something about it."

"Don't you worry," he assured me. "I'm certain someone will clean it up."

Thanking him, I hung up and called a captain who works out of the Tilly Marina. I told him where *Carina* was moored and asked him if he could move her back to the Tilly Marina in West Palm Beach. I wasn't sure how long I'd be gone, but she needed to be somewhere I was sure she'd be looked after.

"Chase!" Rikki called from below. "Come here."

Jumping to my feet, I grabbed the Glock, lying on the helm, and ran downstairs. Rikki was standing in the master stateroom, staring at a metal box lying on the bed. The same chest I brought up when I found the cargo hold on the submarine.

"What's that doing here?" I asked.

She opened the lid to reveal the collection of gold coins with the stamp of the SS.

"I think Wexler brought it in here while you were salvaging the rest," she suggested.

My hand dug into the gold coins and lifted them up, letting the excess spill from my hand. My eyes shifted to see a broad smile on Rikki's face. Her hands wrapped around my cheeks before she pulled me in to kiss me.

The next morning, I dropped anchor just south of Manchionaeal, Jamaica, where we spent a week without ever leaving the boat. The next six weeks found us moving around the island, dropping anchor, and repeating. Eventually, we found our way to shore to dine in the finest of jerk shacks and visit the most remote beaches. We pulled a few crabs and lobster from the bottom, and we spent more time in the stateroom.

When we finished Jamaica, we cut northeast for the Cayman Islands. We spent three more weeks diving and snorkeling along the reefs. The nights we would spend on deck, sipping rum until we emptied the bottle or opted for more strenuous activities below decks.

We didn't think about submarines, gold, or Nazis. Until one morning, I was climbing back aboard after a swim. Rikki was standing at the galley sink, staring at the image of Moses Carter. There was something different.

I kissed her neck, and her hand reached up and stroked my chin.

"You're ready, aren't you?" I asked.

She turned and wrapped her arms around my waist. "Not at all," she lied.

As I cocked my head, I stared at her.

"I mean," she stated, "I don't want to be ready."

"But you are."

She shrugged. "I need to check on Sam."

With a kiss on her forehead, I replied, "I'll tidy up, and we can pull anchor."

She squeezed me tight and offered, "How about we go tomorrow? Tomorrow is a fine day to be ready, isn't it?"

My chin tilted toward hers, and our lips touched.

"Tomorrow is fine."

A week later, we said our goodbyes at the marina in Key West. Rikki was flying up to see Sam at his niece's, and I had to drive back to West Palm. However, there was one stop I wanted to make on the way.

Tali escorted me to the dining room at the Windward Keys Assisted Living Facility. When Jacob Altman entered, he recognized me immediately.

"Where's the pretty one?" he asked.

"She's gone," I told him.

"Happens with the best of them," he remarked with a sly grin. "What brings you here?"

Reaching into my bag, I pulled out a bottle of Angel's Envy Single Barrel Bourbon and set it on the table.

"I thought you might like to hear a story," I offered, sliding a single gold coin across the table to him.

For a list of other books by Douglas Pratt
visit the author's webpage at
http://www.douglas-pratt.com/